# VOYAGE BENEATH
# THE WAVES

Borgo Press Books by JULES RENGADE

*Voyage Beneath the Waves*

# VOYAGE BENEATH THE WAVES

A SCIENCE FICTION NOVEL

## JULES RENGADE

Edited and Translated by Brian Stableford

THE BORGO PRESS

MMXIII

CLASSICS OF
FANTASTIC LITERATURE
NUMBER THIRTEEN

VOYAGE BENEATH THE WAVES

FIRST EDITION

Published by Wildside Press LLC

www.wildsidebooks.com

# CONTENTS

# INTRODUCTION

*Voyage sous les flots, rédige d'après le journal de bord de L'Éclair*, which also bears the heading *Aventures extraordinaires de Trinitus* and the signature Aristide Roger, was first published in book form by "P. Brunet" (Paul Bory) in 1868; it was also serialized in *Le Petit Journal*, beginning in October 1867. The book version was issued in Brunet's Bibliothéque de la Science Pittoresque, and advertised as an exercise in the popularization of science, more specifically as "a fantastic voyage in which the author describes, in an exceedingly curious and interesting fashion, the innumerable marvels of the submarine world."

Jules Verne, who came across the serial version of *Voyage sous les flots* while the serial version of his own *Vingt mille lieues sous les mers* (1870 in book form; tr. as *Twenty Thousand Leagues Under the Sea*) was in preparation, wrote to *Le Petit Journal* in order to make it clear that he had come up with the notion independently of "Aristide Roger"—or, more accurately, of Pierre-Jules Rengade, the author behind that pseudonym—his own story of an underwater voyage having been advertised as forthcoming in P.-J. Hetzel's

*Magasin d'Éducation et de Récréation* in September 1867. Verne probably did that because his sensitivity to such issues had been considerably sharpened by an attempt made to sue him for plagiarism by René de Pont-Jest, on account of similarities between the initiating incident of *Voyage au centre de la terre* (1864; tr. as *Journey to the Centre of the Earth*) and the one featured in his story "La Tête de Miner" (tr. as "Mimer's Head") in the September 1863 issue of the *Revue Contemporaine*.

Pont-Jest had abandoned his suit, presumably persuaded that he could not win it—although he was probably right to assume that Verne had "stolen" his idea of prompting a voyage of exotic discovery to Scandinavia by means of a runic cryptogram—but the incident had been unfortunate. George Sand was later to allege that it was she who had fed the suggestion of writing a novel about an underwater voyage to Hetzel, who had then passed it on to Verne, so Verne was probably correct to feel that people might get the wrong idea if he did not make his position clear.

There was, of course, nothing new about the notion of a submarine, and previous literary use had been made of one by Théophile Gautier in *Les Deux étoiles* (1848; tr. as *The Quartette*), which features a plot to rescue Napoléon from his exile in Saint Helena by that means, but the point at issue was not that Verne's *Nautilus* might seem to have been inspired by Rengade's *Éclair*; the real question was that the wonders of the undersea world that the vessels in question revealed might seem excessively similar. There is, in fact, little similarity between the magnificent *Nautilus* and the rather petty *Éclair*, but it is not surprising that the imagery of the undersea worlds glimpsed by their passengers should have much in common, because the authors were drawing on the same meager resources, not only in terms of the scant knowledge provided by divers and fishermen but in terms of traditional melodramatic potential.

Having made that point, however, the most striking aspect of any comparison made between the two texts is not the similarities due to common research but the differences resulting from Verne's far greater sophistication as a thinker and writer. There was, of course, some direct inspiration involved in the coincidence between the two works, but it was not to do with the machines that provided their central motifs, and the flow of that inspiration was undoubtedly from Verne to Rengade—or, more likely, from Hetzel to Brunet. *Voyage sous les flots* is, in fact, one of the earliest examples of imitative "Vernian fiction," the rapid accumulation of which established Verne's *"voyages extraordinaires"* as a genre rather than an idiosyncratic endeavor. The relative crudity of Rengade's novel also serves to illustrate the fact that, within the genre who creation he had inspired, Verne had an unmatchable talent and intelligence. Other people could do what he was doing, on a prolific scale, but they could not do it anywhere near as well.

The 1860s was a boom period in France for the

popularization of science; there was a rapid prolif-
eration of sections in popular periodicals dedicated
to that task, and several specialist publications were
launched with that objective. One annual of the latter
kind was edited by Samuel Berthoud, a physician who
had been a successful *feuilletonist* twenty years earlier,
and Berthoud made extensive use of fiction in drama-
tizing the history and progress of science, although
only a handful of his works in that vein are specula-
tive. On the other hand, scientists like the astronomer
Camille Flammarion also tried to extend their range
and appeal of their essays by clever fictionalization.
Most such work was a trifle clumsy, because scientific
fact does not lend itself well to fictional transfigura-
tion—as demonstrated by the elaborate newspaper
hoax produced by the pioneering science journalist
Henri de Parville, whose episodes were collected as *Un
Habitant de le planète Mars* (1865; tr. as *An Inhabitant
of the Planet Mars*), most of which simply records the
speeches made at an imaginary scientific conference.

It was probably Hetzel rather than Verne who
decided, before he persuaded Verne to turn a series
of projected articles on ballooning into a novel—
which materialized as *Cinq semaines en ballon* (1863;
tr. as *Five Weeks in a Balloon*)—that the appropriate
strategy was to reverse the priority and write a adventure story in which the various phases of the adventure
might provide hooks on which scientific observations
and discussions could be hung, but that idea was only
one per cent of the genius of Vernian fiction, and it was

Verne's hard labor that provided the other ninety-nine. As *Voyage sous les flots* illustrates very obviously, the strategy was relatively impotent in the absence of the craftsmanship to put it into practice with due artistry. Rengade also demonstrated, as Verne did –again, more successfully—that once the priorities have been reversed, there is a tendency for the popularization of science to fade away entirely, so that the climactic phases of such endeavors become pure and unalloyed melodrama.

*Voyage sous les flots* was by no means a commercial failure, however. The Brunet edition went through half a dozen printings, and the story was given a further lease of life in 1889 when Louis Figuier reprinted a slightly-revised serial version in *La Science Illustrée*, which led to a new book edition—with a preface by the author in which he proudly reprinted Verne's letter, in order to demonstrate his ideative kinship with the great man. The other book of a similar kind that "Aristide Roger" contributed to the series in which *Voyages sous les flots* appeared—*Les Monstres invisibles* [Invisible Monsters] (1868), a fictionalized study of life in the microcosm revealed by microscopy—also went through half a dozen editions, but Rengade made no further attempt to repeat the trick. Brunet advertised a third Aristide Roger title in the series, *La Machine humaine* [The Human Machine], but it did not appear, although Rengade used the title on a series of articles featuring different organs of the body, and it might well be the case that the projected book would simply have been a collection of those articles. Its non-appearance might indicate that Rengade and Brunet had quarreled, but that would not have prevented Rengade from writing more Vernian fiction had he had the urge to do so.

In fact, the only subsequent work of prose fiction that Rengade published after *Les Monstres invisibles* was a naturalistic *roman de moeurs* detailing the exploits of a Parisian physician during the siege of Paris in 1870, *Le Docteur Fabrice* (1888), issued under his own name. He did, however, publish the texts of several plays including a *"revue-féerie en 2 actes et 5 tableaux," Vers l'Avenir!* [Toward the Future], addressed to the workers of the Exposition Universelle of 1900, and he seems to have thought of himself as a writer in the tradition of Molière; one of his endeavors was the one-act comedy *Le Médicin de Molière* (1878). His last works to be published included two advertised under the heading *"roman scénique contemporain"* [contemporary fiction in dramatic form], *Alma mater! Les Victimes de la Sorbonne* (1909) and *La Bête à concours* [The Beast in Competition] (1910).

Like Samuel Berthoud, Rengade was a qualified physician—he always signed his plays "Dr. J. Rengade"—but, unlike Berthoud, he does not seem ever to have practiced medicine after finishing his qualificatory stints as an intern in two Parisian hospitals. Instead, he preferred to follow Parville's example in launching a career as one of the first generation of scientific journalists; he launched a popular periodical of his own in 1867, *La Santé, journal de vulgarisation médicale et scientific* [Health, a magazine of medical and scientific popularization], although it ceased publication a year later. Given that he was a full time professional writer, and that his two exercises in fictional popularization sold so well, it is perhaps surprising that he did not do more in that vein, but it is possible that he simply realized that he could not compete with Verne, and conceded defeat in that particular arena. If the idea of writing *Voyage sous les flots* and *Les Monstres invisibles* had, in fact, been Brunet's rather than Rengade's, it is also possible that Rengade regarded them as mere hackwork, perhaps not entirely unworthy of one Molière's heirs, but nevertheless an occasion for dabbling rather than the adoption of a vocation.

Juxtaposed with *Vingt mille lieues sous les mers, Voyages sous les flots* is certainly a crude affair, especially seen from a contemporary viewpoint, from which its treatment of the natives of Polynesia exhibits all the most unacceptable features of crude racism, but that probably did not work entirely to its disadvantage in terms of appealing to its intended audience. Indeed, its crudity makes it all the clearer as a demonstration of how little was known about the undersea world in 1867. We are so familiar nowadays with the results of sophisticated underwater camera-work that we all know what the world of the sea-bed looks like, in terms of its décor and population, and we also know how difficult it is to see anything at all down there in all but the clearest and calmest of waters, and what vast spaces there are between the surface of the oceans and their abyssal depths. In 1867, however, even the most advanced diving-bells could not go down very far and had not brought back very much in the way of eye-witness accounts, and although the catches of fishermen and other dredgers of the sea-bed had brought back vast numbers of samples of underwater organisms, it was by no means easy to perform the imaginative gymnastics required to envision those specimens in their natural state.

Modern readers know full well that the sea-bed is not brightly illuminated by vast hosts of phosphorescent organisms, that the notion of the weed-choked Sargasso Sea popular in the nineteenth century was more myth than reality, that narwhals do not engage in titanic battles with whales, and that the notion of dangling a trapeze underneath a fast-moving submarine to serve as a viewing platform for men in canvas suits breathing air from the interior of the submarine through long rubber tubes is monumentally silly. The fact that such narrative devices did not seem entirely ridiculous to Rengade and his contemporary readers, however, serves to remind us that the reason that no one prior to 1867 had dared to write a novel about an underwater voyage is that no one had any but the slightest idea of what such a voyage might reveal.

The project was just as difficult, in its own way, as constructing a plausible account of a journey to Mars, whose surface was at least visible to astronomical observation—albeit, as it turned out, somewhat unreliably. Verne's and Rengade's novels were, quite literally, imaginative leaps in the dark, taking their authors and readers into a world in which large-scale imaginative constructions had to be based on woefully inadequate informational foundations. If Rengade went spectacularly awry, he did not do so to a much greater extent than Verne, and the latter writer's enormous literary achievement was more a matter of glossing over his inadequacy of his resources than any spectacular anticipatory success. If Verne did not reproduce all of Rengade's errors in chronicling the exploits of Captain Nemo, that was partly because he had already made many of them before, in *Les Enfants du capitaine Grant*, serialized in the *Magasin d'Éducation et de Récréation* in 1865-67, from which Rengade seems to have borrowed considerable inspiration in shaping his plot—which is, in essence, a brutal abridgement of Verne's, in which the submarine functions as a means of curtailment as well as a vehicle of revelation. (The novel in question was translated into English in three separately-titled volumes, but is best-known nowadays as *In Search of the Castaways*, under which title the story was filmed by Walt Disney's company.)

Both Verne and Rengade deserve credit for taking on the task that they did; it really was a bold attempt to explore the unknown by means of the imagination. The lack of success they enjoyed in terms of accurate prediction of what future underwater exploration would actually reveal is somewhat beside the point; no one can know today what will only be discovered tomorrow. The real issue at stake is whether such journeys are worth undertaking, regardless of the scant chance of predictive success. Verne surely demonstrated that they are, and that entitled him to become the figurehead of an entire genre, which not only collated such attempts but also enabled them to achieve a measure of collective progress. Contrary to what René Pont-Jest thought, it is actually healthy for writers to take inspiration from one another, borrowing one another's ideas in order to extract further mileage from them and exhibit the true breadth of their potential. Mere copying is fruitless, but development is anything but, and although much of the material contained in *Voyage sous les flots* is mere and somewhat inept copying, the narrative does have developmental ambitions, and Brunet and Rengade were correct in their belief that there really was additional mileage to be obtained from jumping on to the Hetzel-Verne bandwagon, in terms of seeing how far it could go, and in what directions.

It is difficult to judge the particular influence of *Voyage sous les flots*, which was bound to be eclipsed by its own model and by its accidental parallels with the serial novel Verne was writing alongside it, but it probably did serve as a significant exemplar to the other writers who soon began to flock to the Vernian banner, including Alphonse Brown, whose own career as a dedicated Vernian was launched in 1875 with *La Conquête de l'air* (1875; tr. as *The Conquest of the Air*), and Albert Robida, whose parodic Vernian fantasy

*Voyages trés extraordinaire de Saturnin Farandoul* (1879; tr. as *The Adventures of Saturnin Farandoul*) surely has *Voyage sous les flots* in mind in one of the key incidents in the first of its five parts, in which the characters witness an undersea battle that results in one of them being carried away and temporarily lost.

Seen from the viewpoint of 1889, let alone from 2013, *Voyage sous les flots* is a historical curiosity, a strange specimen dredged up from the literary deeps, but, just as Louis Figuier was right in thinking that it was worth reprinting then, it is still worth translating now, precisely because it is such a revealing historical illustration. It was, in essence, the first Vernian novel written by someone other than Verne; the novel that demonstrated that the track, once beaten, was well worth treading repeatedly, and that there were potential rewards to be gained from a genre of *voyages extraordinaires* as well as a single series by a single author.

Seen as an adventure story, *Voyage sous les flots* is a cardinal example of what would later be considered to be "pulp fiction"—but that too is illuminating, given that there was not yet any such thing in 1867, which was prior to the advent of the cheap wood-pulp paper that made it possible to produce printed text at a price poor people could afford, thus encouraging the mass-production of fiction aimed at the uneducated and semi-literate. The fact that the novel seems so stereotyped and obsolete now, in its method as well as its content, is partly due to the fact that it was one of the models that helped to create the relevant stereotypes, and to pioneer the melodramatic fashions that were subsequently to become standardized in popular globetrotting action-adventure fiction. It is undoubtedly a bad book, but it is bad in interesting ways, and although it is not a great book, as some bad books are, it is nevertheless a narrative that has virtues, not only in addition to its badness but at their very heart. It is not entirely surprising that it was popular when it was first published in the 1860s, or that it posted a useful signpost for other writers, which Louis Figuier still thought important when he attempted to define, circumscribe and promote the genre of *roman scientifique* two decades later.

This translation was made from the copy of the second Brunet edition reproduced electronically in the Bibliothèque Nationale's *gallica* website.

# CHAPTER ONE
## THE MARVELOUS MACHINE

One Sunday morning, after mass, a man whose face appeared to be imprinted with a bleak sadness was making his way through the crowd in the main square of Calais.

All the people who noticed him looked at him with expressions of profound commiseration; some of them talked to one another about the misfortunes that had overtaken him; others came up to him respectfully to shake his hand and tell him how sorry they were for his troubles.

The man who was the object of so much sympathy was about fifty years old. His talents and inventive genius had won him a reputation for ten leagues around, and although he did not possess any medical qualification no one ever addressed him by any other title than "Doctor Trinitus."

Unfortunately, like many poor and timid inventors. Trinitus had suffered a great deal from the jealousy and bad faith of his rivals. He had almost been financially ruined in trying to realize the machines and items of apparatus that he was incessantly imagining, and the scientific academies of Paris and London had turned a deaf ear to his communications.

The last blow that had struck him had completed his misfortune. His wife Thérèse, the daughter of a rich English family, and his daughter Alice, only eighteen years old, had perished in a shipwreck on their way to collect the immense fortune of a relative who had died six months earlier in Australia.

The insouciance of the English in undertaking long voyages is well-known. Trinitus, retained in France by important work on which he had founded great hopes, had not looked upon the departure of his wife and daughter without great apprehension, but he had been obliged to give in to the pleas and tears of the former and the reckless temperament of the latter.

At any rate, the two voyagers, perhaps driven as much by curiosity as by their financial interests, had departed, under the protection of Thérèse's cousin, Sir William Hervey, the ship's doctor on the *Richmond*, which was to take them to Botany Bay. As far as Timor, where the vessel has refueled, the crossing had been very pleasant, but it seemed that a storm must have assailed the ship in the Coral Sea, for the French steamer *Espérance*, returning from the Marquesas Islands, had discovered the wreckage of the *Richmond* some time afterwards on the coast of an island in the Louisiade Archipelago.

When he heard that terrible news, Trinitus was working mysteriously in his house, situated on the edge of the sea on the road to Gravelines, a short distance from Calais. The mental impact he had sustained was so intense that, for three or four days, it was feared that he might commit suicide in a fit of despair.

For a month he had remained indoors without seeing anyone, only listening to the consolations of Nicaise, a former mariner who had become his gardener, and whom he had adopted as a confidant.

Nicaise had a nephew named Marcel, about twenty-five years old, who was hoping to make a career in the merchant marine. Marcel had long felt a keen affection for Alice, Trinitus' daughter, but, being too poor to aspire to her hand, he had always kept the passion that was devouring him secret. On learning about the wreck of the *Richmond*, he had initially experienced great anguish, but had eventually found in the terrible event a generous idea that gave birth in his heart to a previously-unimagined hope.

Thus, on the Sunday when Trinitus had finally emerged from his house to go to Calais, Marcel, perceiving him in the crowd, hastened to go to him. After having told the scientist how he shared his suffering, he asked him to accord him a few minutes' conversation.

"Would you care to accompany me back to the house?" Trinitus asked him. "You'll be able to see your Uncle Nicaise."

Marcel accepted the offer enthusiastically.

Once they were outside the town, the young man, moved to tears, opened his heart to the scientist. "I've always hidden from you," he told him, "the affection

I experienced for Alice. Our situations were too far apart for me ever to be bold enough to ask you for her hand. If, however, saved by Providence, Alive were still alive, and if I were to have the honor of bringing her back to you one day, would you, in recompense for my devotion, give her to me as a wife?"

Two large tears escaped the scientist's eyes. "Marcel," he said, shaking the young man's hand, "from now on I regard you as my soon. I've resolved to go in search of my child and my beloved Thérèse myself. If you're not afraid to go with me, we can leave in four days."

"In four days! That's impossible…the English steamer doesn't leave London until the end of the month, and it's only the sixteenth today."

"We shan't wait for the steamer."

"But how…?"

"We'll depart in a vessel of my own invention.…"

"A vessel of your invention? To go to Australia?"

"The steamer takes a hundred and ten days to make the journey; we'll only take two weeks."

"What! Two weeks! Did you say two weeks?"

"And we'll travel underwater, like the fish."

On hearing these last words, Marcel uttered a cry of alarm and stopped, amazed.

Trinitus, attempting to smile, looked at him calmly. "I'm not mad," he told him. "You'll see my nutshell, and if you don't have any confidence in her, you can take the steamer.…"

Trinitus' strange proposal was utterly incomprehensible to Marcel. He looked at the scientist with a bewildered expression, not knowing how to respond, and wondering whether it was really possible, rationally, to make such inventions.

*So*, he said to himself, *under the water, in a machine constructed by this man, we're going to go from Calais to Australia, in the middle of Oceania? The very idea is insane! We're two madmen, the scientist and I!*

While devoting himself to these reflections, however the young man continued walking alongside Trinitus.

After an hour they arrived at the house and were greeted by Nicaise. The master of the house went to fetch the keys to his laboratory.

In the meantime, Marcel stayed in the garden with his uncle. "Tell me frankly," he said to him, "is the doctor's mind a little deranged?"

"Get away! You're joking. Why do you ask?"

"He wants to take me to Australia, under water, in a fortnight...."

Bewildered, Nicaise looked his nephew in the face. "What are you saying?" he said, dazedly.

"He's built a boat capable of doing that...come on, you must know something about it?"

"A boat, you say? Hang on!" Nicaise's face suddenly lit up. "For ten years we've been working on something of which I've only seen the separate parts. The doctor has assembled the machine himself, in secret, keeping it hidden in the big room adjacent to his laboratory. That must be the boat!"

At that moment Trinitus emerged from the house carrying a bunch of keys and headed toward the outbuilding in which he had set up his laboratory.

"Come on," he said to Marcel, and then added: "You too, Nicaise.…"

He opened the door of his workshop, then that of the large room into which only he had entered for ten years, and he invited Nicaise and is nephew to come in. The intense darkness prevented anything from being discernible.

"I'll switch the light on," said Trinitus.

Immediately, four beams of light, as bright and dazzling as that of the sun, sprang from the four corners of the room. Marcel and his uncle, inundated by the glare, stepped back to the doorway, and uttered a double exclamation of surprise and admiration.

An enormous machine in shiny copper, as voluminous as a railway carriage, occupied the center of the room, which it partly filled. It was shaped like an immense egg, slightly flattened underneath and at the sides. Four large portholes made of extremely thick sheets of glass were integrated into its walls. As many large pallets, similar to fins, emerged from its flanks, and beneath the rudder set at the rear, the unparalleled boat was fitted with a helical propeller.

Marcel and Nicaise, their hands pressed together and their mouths open, gazed at the monstrosity.

Trinitus, proud of the astonishment into which they had been plunged, opened one of the portholes and climbed up on the footplate that had just been lowered therefrom.

"This is our carriage," he said. "Come and look

inside."

The three men went into the machine and descended on to a horizontal floor set about forty centimeters below the widest diameter.

The interior side-walls, made of sheet metal coated with gutta-percha, extended like a dome overhead. A multitude of rings, buttons, knobs, each connected to some ingenious mechanism, protruded at various heights. Trinitus pointed them out to the two visitors.

"The whole secret of its control is there," he told them. Then, indicating the floor, he added: "The engine producing the motive force of the boat is beneath our feet. It consists of enormous electric piles, furnishing a considerable quantity of electricity: large coils, a hundred times more powerful than Ruhmkorff's. With the aid of the handle you can see over there, we can control them at our ease. By pressing the button alongside, we can light the electric lamp suspended overhead. By lifting up the trap-door that opens in the middle of the floor we can descend into the sea as easily as by means of a diving-bell, without a single drop of water getting into the ship. You'll see that later.

"At present, take note of that iron rod protruding from the interior extremity of the vessel. It goes through the wall and projects a spike about three meters long outside. It's an intelligent prow. When it strikes an obstacle, it recoils slightly, presses on a small spring, and the electricity immediately acts in a contrary direction; the ship retreats abruptly, in order to escape the danger. There's no possibility of an accident. The windows, as you can see, are arranged in such a fashion that one can see what's happening on all sides, and even above the boat.

"The hull, which is extremely solid, caused me a great deal of difficulty. It's more than twenty meters thick, and yet it's very light. Lined with copper externally, it's formed of a primary envelope of oak, a layer of rubber ten centimeters thick, a second envelope of oak and a plate of metal covered in gutta-percha.

"This, my dear Marcel, is the whole of what I have to offer you...."

The dazzled young man could have believed that he was in the power of an enchanter. The extraordinary machine seemed to him to be the work of a supernatural being. "Doctor," he exclaimed, "Do with me as you will; I'm ready to follow you to the ends of the earth!"

Nicaise, however, who had learned to respect the dangers and caprices of the sea in his childhood, was not as easily enthused as his nephew by Trinitus' "fishboat." A host of objections was crowding his skull, making him dread that the scientist's dream was incapable of realization.

So, when the latter had concluded his explanations, the old mariner, shaking his head, said to him with assurance: "If I didn't know you, Monsieur Trinitus, I'd think that the Devil had something to do with your machine—but I don't believe that it will ever take you where you want to go."

"Why is that, if you please, Master Nicaise?" the

scientist asked.

"Because your boat is no bigger than a pill, and the tempest will swallow it whole."

"Even the most violent tempest only agitates the sea to a feeble depth. It will rumble over our heads, but will never stir the layers of water through which we're traveling."

"Good idea—but is it only to be sheltered from tempests that you've devised this submarine boat?"

"Certainly not; it's also in order not to have to worry about the wind, the tides, mists and fogs. I've constructed it with the thought that it might enable me to accomplish a strange voyage of which I've always dreamed...."

"Really?" said Marcel.

"Yes. I wanted, with this boat, to reach and traverse the North Pole, passing under the ice...."

"My God!" cried Nicaise. "You're not afraid of anything! But merciful Heaven, when you're at the bottom of the sea, enclosed in this calabash, how the devil will you get back up to the surface again?"

"Nicaise, my friend, have you never watched a fish swim? It has various ways of inclining and moving its fins, which permit it to move forwards or backwards, to maintain itself in equilibrium, to rise or descend— in brief, to move in every direction. Now, the pallets of my boat are nothing but fins. The nervous fluid that moves the organs of the fish is the electric fluid that makes my pallets function as I wish. What more do you want?"

"If you say so! But that's not all. On what will you live in your prison?"

"On the food that we'll take with us. It's very nutritious in low doses, such as compressed beef, the meat extract prepared by the chemist Liebig,[1] broth in tablet form, and so on."

"And where will you get drinkable water?"

"We'll restock sometimes; in addition, we'll distill sea water, of which we'll have plenty."

"Yes, perhaps, but I'm still unconvinced. How will you breathe? You'll run out of air very quickly."

"My dear Nicaise, that problem was resolved a long time ago. We'll manufacture air...."

"Get away! Is that possible?"

"It's child's play. Air is made up of two gases, oxygen and nitrogen. They both penetrate the lungs together when we breathe, but only the oxygen in absorbed. The nitrogen comes out again as it went in; in consequence, the same quantity can serve indefinitely. It's inexhaustible. Thus, we have only to attend to the manufacture of oxygen, and we have a hundred methods at our disposal. We could ourselves to decomposing potassium chlorate by means of heat; however, as we'd need to expend ten pounds of that salt per day, I thought that we ought also to have recourse to the decomposition of water by electricity. The oxygen obtained by that method will permit us to save three or four pounds of potassium chlorate per day, which isn't to be disdained from the viewpoint of the loading of the boat.

1. The meat extract produced by Justus von Liebig's Meat Extract Company, founded in 1865, was eventually trademarked as "Oxo."

"Furthermore, the decomposition of water by the pile will give us another very precious gas, because it can be burned to produce heat—that's hydrogen. We'll collect it separately and make use of it for heating and cooking. That's it, as regards the manufacture of gases, but it's not just a matter of creating them continuously; it's also necessary to give some thought to their destruction.

"In our atmosphere, thus composed, we shall have an enemy, carbon dioxide, exhaled by the lungs. Oh well, it will be easy to get ride of it; we shall drown it in a solution of caustic potash. Carbon dioxide, having a very pronounced appetite for potassium, will precipitate itself thereinto of its own accord, and we'll thus obtain a new chemical product, potassium carbonate, which might be useful to us on occasion."

While Trinitus was talking, Nicaise's face cleared rapidly. The theory of the manufacture of air had convinced him completely. "I've only one more thing to ask you, Doctor," he said. "Will you permit me to go with you?"

"So you're no longer afraid of tempests?"

"I don't say that…but if we run into trouble *en route*, I know now that you'll invent a machine that will take us straight to paradise."

"Well then, join us. We're leaving in four days, and we'll start equipping the ship this evening."

"Agreed! Things were no different in the time of fairy tales."

"Fairies no longer exist today, my dear Nicaise.

The good fairy is named Science and the bad one Ignorance."

"Then let's depart without fear!" exclaimed Marcel. "The good fairy is with us!"

Thanks to the feverish activity of Trinitus and his companions, the equipment of every sort necessary to the submarine voyage were loaded into the boat in three days.

Two special bunkers received the food-supplies. A complete laboratory of chemistry and photography was enclosed in a large trunk, along with ropes, glass and rubber tubing of various dimensions, and the instruments most useful to carpenters and mechanics.

Firearms, including two rifles, three shotguns and three six-shot revolvers, were suspended from the walls of the vessel. A crate lined with iron enclosed gunpowder, bullets and a few packets of lead shot.

A table surmounted by two shelves was placed in the vessel's anterior concavity. On the shelves, Trinitus arranged the apparatus designed for the manufacture of oxygen, both by the decomposition of water and that of potassium chlorate. He also put the receptacle for hydrogen gas there and the jars containing caustic potash, reserving the table for chemical and culinary operations.

Finally, under the table he deposited all the fishing equipment and three-diving suits, indispensable to the travelers for descending from their boat into the sea.

At the other extremity of the cabin, below the lever controlling the rudder, next to the compass, Trinitus placed another small table, which served as a desk for a portable compass, a sextant, and excellent microscope, a few books and several large maps of the Atlantic and Oceania. He also suspended a mercury barometer at that location, and three good thermometers for the air and for the water.

Two folding chairs, two hammocks and a basket containing a few clothes completed the ship's equipment.

All the preparations having been completed, the departure was set for the next day, at nightfall.

The excited voyagers met up again at two o'clock in the afternoon in Trinitus' house. The scientist had spent the morning loading the enormous Daniel piles that were to power the boat with acidulated copper sulfate, and he had checked all his calculations one last time.

When Nicaise and Marcel presented themselves, dressed in woolen clothes and shod in tarred gaiters, the skillful technologist shook their hands effusively, and could not help a tear rolling down his cheek.

"My dear friends," he said, "You have no fear of exposing yourselves, with me, to the thousand dangers that might perhaps await us; let me express all my gratitude, and to regard you from now on as beloved brothers."

Nicaise and Marcel, their hearts swelling, stammered a few words and went back in with the scientist.

It had been decided that they would eat dinner before leaving, but their emotion was stronger than their appetite. At table, they only talked about the voyage, and especially the dear absentees of whom they were going in search.

Nicaise reminisced about the good Madame Thérèse; he recalled her excellent qualities one by one, saying how gentle, charitable and generous she was.

Marcel, for his part, spoke admiringly about Alice. What a charming child! What pretty eyes she had! What beautiful blonde hair! What a gracious smile!

Trinitus only contrived a few remarks through his tears. Where were they now, those poor beloved women? Had they survived the shipwreck? Perhaps, alas, fallen into the hands of some savage tribe, they were enduring the most atrocious torments!

At that terrible thought, the scientist's face took on an expression of the most profound dolor. His fists clenched convulsively. He became annoyed with himself for not having left yet.

However, as dusk gradually fell, the three men got up, locked up the house and went to the laboratory.

Trinitus opened a huge door with two battens, separated from the sea by a terrace about thirty meters broad, and the scientist's two companions understood that it was only necessary to push the machine to set it afloat immediately.

"The way is open!" said Trinitus. "There are little wheels under the boat; we only have to push...."

"Come on, hard!" exclaimed Nicaise, and ran forward to be the first to lean on the propeller to launch the ship."

"Off we go!" replied Trinitus and Marcel.

Immediately, a kind of frenzy took hold of the three travelers. The boat, pushed out of the laboratory with an incredible energy, traversed the terrace and slid gently on to the surface of the waves....

Marcel and Nicaise, transported by enthusiasm, uttered a cry of admiration and surprise, and even Trinitus stood still momentarily in amazement.

"It's splendid!" he cried.

At that moment, in fact, the moon illuminated the dome of the machine, making it shine like a ruby sphere, and the sky, reflected in the glass of its port-holes, was reproduced there with its thousands of stars.

"I'll embark first!" said Marcel.

"You next, Nicaise," said Trinitus.

"I'd like that—but before then, I want to baptize the ship."

"So be it!" said the scientist.

"Let's call her the *Éclair*, since lightning is powering her."

"That name suits her marvelously. We'll make twenty-five leagues an hour, and tomorrow evening, God willing, we'll be in the Azores...."

# CHAPTER TWO
## AT SEA

When Nicaise had taken his place in the boat beside Marcel, Trinitus went inside in his turn, carefully sealed the porthole and put his hand on the lever that served to direct the electric current into the mechanisms of the ship.

"No one will miss the land?" he asked.

"No, no—let's go," replied Nicaise and Marcel, simultaneously.

"Well, may God preserve us!" exclaimed Trinitus.

There was a slight shock; the lamp fixed in the ceiling of the cabin suddenly projected a bright light, and the *Éclair* shot across the surface of the waves with the rapidity of a shooting star traversing the sky.

"We're flying like a swallow!" said Nicaise.

"Not yet," Trinitus replied, "but we'll travel much faster under water. I'm trying to reach the middle of the Channel. There are two sand-banks to avoid: the Varne Bank, where the Dutch three-master *Maria Jacoba* ran aground a few years ago; and the Colbart Bank, which is no less dangerous...."

"How will you navigate?" asked Marcel.

"By means of the lighthouse on Cap Gris-Nez, which I can see through the window," the scientist replied.

"I can see it too," said Nicaise, "and I think that we ought to be level with the Colbart Bank now."

"That's my opinion...let's go a little bit further...."

"There—now!"

"We're there. Pay attention...."

"One moment!" said Marcel, hastening to the window that looked out upon France.

The boat stopped, and the three voyagers turned their gazes toward the gray and misty ribbon that limited the southern horizon.

"This is it!" murmured Marcel, sighing.

Trinitus' eyes filled with tears. Nicaise felt, to his surprise, that his heart was beating faster.

"What is it?" he said. "I've almost drowned twenty times over; I've been frozen fishing for cod off the coast of Iceland; I've fought polar bears without ever flinching, and now I go weak! Come on, come on— let's light a pipe and get on with it!"

No matter how much effort he made to master his emotion, however, the old mariner allowed a tear to leak from his eye when Trinitus shook his hand and said to him: "I'm hopeful, Nicaise, that our wishes will be granted. We'll find my dear Thérèse and my beloved Alice! I have a feeling that tells me so. If anything bad were going to happen to us, the sky would not have that purity—a good augury, which inspires me and revives my courage!"

The sky was, indeed, displayed in all its splendor

that evening. Not one cloud could be seen; the moon and stars had never shone more brightly. The sea, ordinarily choppy off the Pas-de-Calais, was calm and tranquil; it had doubtless come to an understanding with the sky. Only a few soft and tender waves swayed the boat very slightly at intervals, and their crests could be seen breaking in the distance, emitting a pale phosphorescent light.

A cool breeze was running through the atmosphere.

Two great dark spaces opened to the west and the east. On one side was the entrance to the Channel, on the other that of the North Sea. On the English and French coasts, the lighthouses projected the brilliant beams of their occulting lights a long way out to sea. They could make out quite clearly, on one side, the lights of Dover and Folkestone, and on the other, those of Calais and Cap Gris-Nez.

The upper hemisphere of Trinitus' boat emerged from the middle of the waves, and the bright light illuminating the interior escaped through the portholes in long silvery beams, which vacillated softly on the ridges of the waves.

Having darted one last glance at the coast that they might never seen again, the three voyagers decided to go down to the bottom of the sea. Trinitus put his hand on a ring fixed to the wall and pulled it vigorously toward him. The pallets that were supporting them on the surface of the water assumed a vertical stance and the boat sank softly into the abyss.

The sea allowed her to plunge into its depths. It

swallowed her up beneath its waves, and closed insouciantly over her.

As the ship went down, the scientist's eyes followed the ascension of a thin column of liquid in a vertical tube placed in the floor of the cabin.

"That's our manometer," he said. "The lower extremity of this graduated tube opens into the sea. The further we descend, the greater the pressure exerted on us will be. I've calculated that for every twenty meters of depth, the column of liquid in the manometer will rise one degree. We'll soon be at forty-five meters; we'll be able to maintain ourselves there."

"Very good!" said Nicaise. "I believe that we'll get by without any encumbrance—and without crushing anyone!"

Trinitus pushed the mechanism that he had pulled back toward the wall, forcefully. Almost instantaneously, the boat ceased sinking and moved off horizontally, with an extreme rapidity.

At that moment, the *Panthère*, which was operating a service between Boulogne and London via the Thames, was going through the narrowest part of the Channel. The passengers grouped on the deck saw a strange light fleeing beneath them. A naturalist affirmed that it was produced by medusas, gelatinous mollusks phosphorescent by night, and everyone believed him.

It was Trinitus' boat!

Meanwhile, the ship had scarcely got under way when its skillful pilot was already occupied in organizing the interior duty roster, and giving his companions their share of the work.

Marcel, having youth and intelligence in his favor, became the scientist's assistant. He was charged with supervising the manufacture of artificial air, maintaining the piles and coils, and looking after the precision instruments and weapons of every kind.

Nicaise had nothing to envy Molière's famous Maître Jacques.[2] He was occupied with the fishing tackle, the food, the cooking and the emergency apparatus, as well as the general order of the boat.

Trinitus, the captain and pilot, reserved the direction of the *Éclair* for himself—and, indeed, he alone was capable of fulfilling that role.

Meanwehile, the boat was traveling at top speed. The emotion that had saddened the voyagers slightly at the moment of departure disappeared slowly; they felt their joyful enthusiasm and all their hopes revive.

Marcel never ceased dreaming about Alice, glimpsing a corner of paradise in the future. Nicaise, proud of his appointment as cook, tried to remember various recipes for seamen's court-bouillons, and hummed the tune of *"Marlbrough s'en vat-t-en guerre"* gaily. It was his favorite song.

As for Trinitus, after he had assigned everyone his duties, he went to his desk, checked the time on his chronometer, and on the first page of a notebook opened in front of him, he wrote:

---

2. Maître Jacques is Harpagon's cook in *L'Avare* [The Miser] (1668)

## THE ÉCLAIR
### Submarine Boat

*Departed Calais for the Coral Sea midnight,*
*3 August 1864*

Then, at the bottom of the page, he added:

*Journal of Captain Trinitus.*

As he finished writing, however, an extremely violent shock made the boat shake. The *Éclair* recoiled abruptly, and the three surprised men were hurled on to the floor.

Nicaise only had the strength to utter an oath.

Marcel, alarmed, exclaimed: "We're doomed!"

Stupefied, Trinitus did not make a sound.

Nothing alarming was manifest, however. The boat had stopped, but the damage did not appear to be considerable.

"I understand," said Tirintus, getting up. "We've run into a projection of the sea-bed."

"We need to check the hull for damage," added Nicaise.

"I won't deny that I was very scared," said Marcel.

"You're not used to it yet," said Nicaise.

"The sea isn't as deep here as I thought," Trinitus went on, putting on a diving-suit. We're only at forty-five meters, and throughout the Channel, soundings give at least fifty meters of depth. I can't explain the accident."

The scientist lifted a circular trap-door set in the middle of the floor, uncovering a metal disk about sixty centimeters in diameter. The disk was exactly fitted to a vertical cylinder that traversed the entire keel and terminated at the inferior face of the boat. Four stout tubes descended in parallel with it, but they were open at the top, and projected by about ten centimeters at the bottom, where there was a kind of fitment sealed by a tap.

Trinitus took advantage of the opportunity to inform his friends regarding the mechanism of that ingenious apparatus, and when they understood it in theory he showed them how it worked in practice.

By means of a little pulley fixed in the vault of the boat, he connected the metal disk to a counterweight, and the cylinder immediately opened, like that of a pump when the piston is withdrawn. Trinitus, dressed in his diving-suit, descended into the cylinder and the disk fell back slowly over his head to shut the scientist in, as if in a casket. But he pressed a little switch set in the wall of his narrow prison, causing a valve that closed the lower orifice of the cylinder to open beneath his feet, and slid into the sea.

The valve closed abruptly, after the metal disk had descended level with it, in order to prevent the water from getting in.

Meanwhile, Trinitus had grabbed a handle placed under the vessel for that express purpose, and while supporting himself thus with one hand, he fixed a long flexible hose at the other extremity, by means of which he could breathe through one of the stout tubes that projected out from beneath the ship. By turning the tap, he put himself in communication with the air contained in the cabin, and that played the role of diving-bell.

The respiratory hose of the apparatus was about thirty meters long, which permitted Trinitus to walk along the sea-bed to investigate the obstacle with which the *Éclair* had collided.

Even on the darkest nights, it is never pitch-dark under the sea. The phosphorescence of the water casts a vague light over submerged objects, and the majority of marine animals and plants are surrounded by a phosphoric aureole. Trinitus was therefore able to perceive in front of him a kind of enormous barrier coated with bizarre incrustations and strange vegetation, which projected a pale light over it. He approached it, thinking that he was looking at the mast of a ship, and uttered a cry of surprise.

Suddenly, Nicaise and Marcel heard an exclamation resonating in the cabin. "My friends! It's the electric cable!"[3]

One can imagine the astonishment of the two men when they learned that the obstacles with which they had collided was none other than the enormous iron cable that is the sole link attaching us to England.

Curious to descend to the bottom of the sea, they

---

3. The first telegraphic cable linking England and France was laid between Dover and Calais in 1850 by John Watkins Brett and his brother. It had to be replaced in 1851 with an armored version after a French fisherma cut the first one.

promptly put on their apparatus. Marcel applied his lips to the orifice of the tube through which Trinitus was breathing, and shouted at the top of his voice: "Wait there! We're coming!"

Ignorant of the simplest laws of physics, Marcel did not know that it was sufficient for him to speak in a normal voice for Trinitus to hear him; thus, in his impermeable prison, the scientist was stunned by the brutal exclamation that fell upon him so loudly. His ears were still ringing when his two companions, linked like him to the machine by respiratory tubes, appeared at his sides.

"What a strange place!" said Niciase.

"It's magnificent!" said Marcel.

"Why," the old mariner continued, "once can see here as if by gaslight. Is there moonlight under the sea?"

"No, Nicaise," Trinitus replied. "It's the objects surrounding us that are producing this strange light. You're already lit up in the darkness like a box of matches."

"So the gleam that's illuminating us is the same one that sometimes shines on the waves at night?"

"Exactly. It's caused by animalcules that I'll show you under the microscope in a little while. They exist in such great numbers in the sea that there are more than a million of them in a single drop of water. They're known as *Noctiluca...*."

"Oh, my God, is it possible?" exclaimed Nicaise.

"It's very curious," Marcel added.

Although they were only a few meters from one another, it would have been impossible for them to talk to one another directly because of the glass helmets that were imprisoning them, but they were able to converse because their voices rose up through the respiratory tube of the speaker, resounded in the cabin and came back down the listeners' neighboring tubes, quite clearly and without distortion.

Marcel had approached the electric cable and was contemplating the extravagant vegetation it bore with profound amazement. An incredible multitude of living things were fixed on the submerged cord—which, resting on submarine rocks at intervals, formed a kind of suspension bridge between them. The algae, zoophytes, mollusks and polyps attached to that frail point of support had no suspicion that human speech was running beneath their feet every day. Entangled with one another, they were grouped into enormous bouquets, transforming the cable into an enormous tufted garland barring the Ocean.

Undulating *Laminaria* that were reminiscent of gigantic gladioli were sparkling like flaming swords. *Zonaria* deployed their sumptuous foliage in fans, richer in brilliant gleams than a peacock's tail; *Fucus* and *Plocamia* bore an infinite quantity of sea-shells, like gold and silver fruits striped with the most vivid colors, at the extremities of their stems. Beside a mass of phosphorescent sponges, sea-anemones blossomed; further away, *Ophiura* spread their bristling arms, like enormous millipedes, and *Campanularia* vibrated gently, like flowers attempting to detach themselves gradually from their stems.

That entire mysterious society dwelt in the most profound security. There were inexplicable creatures there whose exterior was plant-like and interior animal-like; and there were others that, like certain fabulous monsters, had flesh bodies supported by feet of stone.

Nicaise and Trinitus, having observed that the boat had been slightly dented by the violent impact it had received, finally joined Marcel in contemplating the picturesque flora of the electric cable.

Suddenly, Nicaise uttered a cry of joy. He had just bumped into a formless mass, and, on bending down to look at it, had found that he and his companions were walking over an oyster-bed.

"Pick them up!" he exclaimed. "Pick them up! Here's our dinner!"

As strokes of good luck never happen in isolation, however, Nicaise while rummaging under rocks covered in the precious bivalves, was dexterous enough to grab hold of a spider-crab and a sea-urchin. He plunged them into the large tarred canvas bag that he had fitted to his apparatus, and buried them with three or four dozen oysters.

"Let's go back!" aid Trinitus. "It's time to go."

"What a pity," Marcel replied. "Can't we travel like this, in our apparatus, without shutting ourselves away in the cabin?"

"What an idea!" said Trinitus.

"It seems to me," Marcel continued, "that nothing

would be simpler. It would be sufficient to fit a kind of swing under the boat, on which one could sit, while the *Éclair* traveled at top speed...."

"That's true—we'd have a better view of the country," added Nicaise.

"Well, my lads, we'll see about that," Trinitus replied. "As regards breakfast, though, it's still necessary to go back into the cabin—we can talk about Marcel's project while eating our oysters!"

Immediately, the three voyagers hoisted themselves up to the ship, and Nicaise, laden with the booty, went in first. Trinitus carefully reclosed the opening of the cylinder; the cook went to his oven in order to prepare the crab and the sea-urchin, and Marcel visited the apparatus for manufacturing air.

The boat, which had only sustained insignificant damage as a result of the collision, set off again with frightful speed, and the captain recorded the first incident that had occurred in his journal.

The breakfast was excellent, and Marcel's proposal, after mature reflection, was accepted unanimously. It was decided that three seats on a plank would be suspended beneath the vessel, in the fashion of a swing, and that each passenger would be armed with a long barbed harpoon for self-defense.

That was not sufficient for Nicaise, however; he wanted to have a more formidable weapon against the large marine animals that would not fail to present themselves, and Trinitus was obliged to invent a kind of thunderbolt with which to kill them.

He devised a kind of iron arrow, which a long metallic chain would connect to the boat's electrical apparatus. A small steel hammer, sustained by a spring, would serve to change the direction of the current and make a quantity of electricity large enough to kill an enormous shark instantly to pass into the arrow through the intermediary of the chain.

The apparatus was, moreover, easy to construct. Trinitus had the principal components in his stores, and in the Azores, where they would have to pause in order to repair the boat, they would obtain the luxury of a small thunderbolt in no time.

Nicaise and Marcel then started rooting through the storage-lockers and gathering together everything they might need. In the meantime, Trinitus drew up all the details of the thunderbolt as he imagined it, and calculated its effects theoretically, which awaiting an opportunity to take account of them in reality.

The entire morning was devoted to that important work, and during the rest of day, Trinitus, in accordance with his promise, told his companions the story of some of the bizarre creatures that they had seen on the sea-bed.

To begin with, he showed them, under the microscope, the animalcule that produces the phosphorescence of the waves. It was a tiny creature, triangular in form, bearing a slender fin at reach of its angles, formed of extremely delicate threads. On its globular back, a host of little spherical dots could be seen, distributed at random, which shone at times with a bright gleam.

The phenomenon was produced most strikingly when Trinitus caressed the *Noctiluca*'s threads with the point of a needle, or teased the animal slightly.

Then the scientist introduced his companions to several extremely curious zoophytes that he had removed from the electric cable or collected on the nearby rocks. He showed them starfish with pink limbs; sponges and *Thetis* clad with their polyps, gray *Pennatula* that resembled silky and curly feathers; and *Eleutheria*, the numerous arms of which were each terminated by a flower.

What amused Marcel most, however, was a kind of Holothurian, Duvernoy's *Synapta*, thus baptized by Monsieur de Quatrefages,[4] who had first observed it in the little archipelago of Chausey abut thirty years before. Trinitus explained how the *Synapta* tolerated famine and abstinence philosophically. Its body, as transparent as crystal, contracts and segments with the greatest ease. In times of famine, when it is impossible to nourish its entire body, the *Synapta* does not hesitate to sacrifice itself in small portions as the necessity becomes apparent. It shrinks, strangling itself at the place where it wants to cut through itself, and gradually diminishes thus by a quarter, a half and three-quarters. Sometimes, alas, it only retains its head, and is very glad when it can find something to eat.

As the day went by, however, the *Éclair* continued traveling toward the Azores. When night fell and

---

4. The zoologist Armand de Quatrefages de Bréau (1810-1892) had been a pupil of Georges Louis Duvernoy (1777-1855). His paper on the "Synapte de Duvernoy" was published in 1841.

Trinitus calculated that the islands could not be far away, he took the boat up to the surface, which slowed its progress considerably but allowed the voyagers to interrogate the horizon through the windows.

The sea extended in all directions, seemingly infinite. Its high and rapid waves shook the boat forcefully, and after half an hour of continual shocks, Trinitus was on the point of deciding to go back down to calmer layers when Marcel saw an almost-imperceptible light shining on the horizon. It looked to him like a kind of gray needle outlined against the wan background of the sky, in which numerous stars were twinkling, and he thought he recognized the mast of a vessel.

Nicaise, whose sight was rather weak, could not make anything out, even with the aid of a powerful telescope, but Trinitus, on seeing the needle identified by Marcel uttered a cry of joy.

"Land! Land, my friends! It's the volcanic peak of the Azores; we'll have disembarked within the hour."

# CHAPTER THREE
## THE AZORES

If you examine the vast blue expanse that separates the old world from the new on a terrestrial globe, you will see that it is dotted here and there with small groups of islands, which appear to be the summits of submarine mountains.

These flocks are most numerous in the north Atlantic, and the most apparent of all, because it is the most distant from the neighboring continents, is that of the Azores.

The majority of the Atlantic islands are volcanic in origin. They emerge from the midst of the waves.

The sea-bed rests directly on the immense globe of fire placed in the center of the Earth, and only forms a floor of very feeble thickness between the two abysms that it separates. It supports the Atlantic, and covers an ocean of minerals in fusion. Those two gigantic powers have been in conflict since the beginning of the world. The enormous liquid mass weighs upon the colossal furnace and maintains it by the crushing weight of its waves. In vain the ocean of fire inflates, swells up, and strives against the thin layer that masters it; its adversary paralyzes it and overwhelms it with its victorious pressure, as barbarians once stifled the enemies they had vanquished under their bucklers.

In that continual and formidable combat, the Ocean bed is sometimes agitated by mighty shocks. Its quakes and trepidations resound as far as the continents, and occasionally, at certain points, it cracks and opens.

Then, through a gaping fissure, the subterranean fire erupts—but the implacable Ocean opposes it. It pours into the breach and exhausts itself driving back the torrent of flames that rises up into it. The impact of the two adversaries is terrible. Like two furious tigers, attacking one another, they roar and rend one another. On contact with the column of fire, the sea boils, seethes and rises up. It tramples its enemy, growling with rage and dolor. There is a terrible battle between the water and the red-hot lava.

That prodigious mass of incandescent matter cannot always be extinguished and cooled by the Ocean. It rises up slowly beneath the weight that it supports, gradually climbing, invading the domain of the sea and suddenly overflows into the submarine plains and valleys. Like an immense fiery polyp, the volcano elongates enormous tentacles of lava around its monstrous mouth; the water hisses and vaporizes on contact with them; those sinuous arms undulate and reach out, as if to seize the Ocean in a horrible embrace.

In vain the latter continues the desperate struggle. It plunges furiously into the depths of the volcano to stifle it; the volcano drinks it in and spits it out. From the bosom of the crater escape swirls of ashes and burning pumice, which soil and thicken the waves; immense gaseous bubbles part the waves and lift them up, cleaving a path to the atmosphere; waters charged with sulfur boil, and their asphyxiated inhabitants drift with the masses of ash and scoria.

After the battle, when the weary volcano has died down, one can see in the place it occupied a submarine mountain. It is sealed by the lava that the crater has vomited forth; they are the foundations of an island. In a more or less distant time, the combat will resume, perhaps more terrible than before; the mountain will rise up further. Until the mouth of the volcano opens directly into the atmosphere, the frightful struggles will succeed one another.

Then, for many years, the crater will vomit lava, ash and thick vapors. One day, however, it will end up going out, and the winds will carry seeds stolen from the soil of neighboring continents to its sterile flanks. Birds of passage will pause on its rocks; seagulls will build their nests there; the sun will nourish a rich vegetation on its hills; springs of fresh water will emerge from its steep slopes to fertilize its plains and valleys.

The young and cheerful island will have its own atmosphere and climate. In its first spring it will be astonished to feel life germinating in its loins; in summer it will be proud of its ornamentation with flowers; in autumn it will shiver with pleasure at the sight of the red fruits it will have nourished; and in winter, when snow covers the blunted summit of the former crater, it will fall asleep peacefully to the sound of the waves, which will come, vanquished and submissive, to break on its shores.

Such has been the origin of the volcanic islands of the Atlantic and all the other oceans that bathe our globe. The central fire has given birth to them in strenuous labor.

The archipelagos of the Canaries, Cape Verde Islands and the Azores had been completed long before humans discovered them; even so, they sometimes experience violent earthquakes, and phenomena often observed in their vicinity demonstrate that the forces that gave birth to them are still at work. These islands, daughters of Water and Fire, have only been known for some four centuries.

The ancients, fully persuaded that the world ended at the Pillars of Hercules, nowadays prosaically known as the Strait of Gibraltar, had scarcely any notion of the Atlantic, which they insulted with the name of the Ocean River. The Canaries, neighbors of the west coast of Africa, had been perceived by their boldest navigators, but they were regarded as an extraordinary land; Elysium was placed there, the abode of the blessed, and poets celebrated them as the Fortunate Isles. Madeira, which had been glimpsed in the distance, passed for a deceptive mist, and the Cape Verde Islands, the existence of which was suspected subsequently, were baptized the Garden of the Hesperides.

Beyond Elysium, it was said, an immense country extended, which was named Atlantis, and was described by Plato. It was in the place where the Sargasso Sea extends today, so encumbered by algae that ships have difficult forcing a passage through it.

As for the Azores, they were completely unknown. An old tradition attributes their discovery to the Arabs, but it was not until 1432 that Gonzalo Velho Cabral identified the island of Santa Maria and took possession of it in the name of Portugal. The other islands—São Miguel, Terceira, Graciosa, São Jorge, Picot, Faial, Flores and Corvo—were discovered successively between 1423 and 1450, but it is said that the first colonists who disembarked on Corvo found an equestrian statue there. The strange individual it represented was pointing westwards, a few authors say, as if to advertise the existence of the New World; others, by contrast, claim that it was instructing navigators to return whence they came.

At any rate, since 1450 the Azores have gradually been populated, and they now have 180,000 inhabitants. The majority are of Portuguese origin; although isolated in the middle of the Ocean, on a land that often experiences convulsions, they live a placid and happy existence. The impatient and feverish soil that they cultivate furnishes abundant crops and exquisite wines.

The peak of Azores is the culminating point of the archipelago. Its summit is almost always covered in snow, and a plume of heavy vapors sometimes still floats there. On its own, it constitutes almost the entirety of the island of Pico.

It was at the base of that mountain that Trinitus decided to stop. It was about four o'clock in the morning, and day was breaking with the boat reached the coast. In order not to be pestered by curiosity-seekers, the *Éclair* was taken into a small bay surrounded by rocks and veiled by bushy trees. The three voyagers disembarked, and Nicaise moored the boat securely.

In the morning, Trinitus left his companions in order to go to the nearest village to have the blacksmith prepare a few pieces of iron destined for the thunderbolt machine whose construction was planed. In the meantime, Marcel and Nicaise repaired the hull of the *Éclair* with considerable intelligence.

When that work was finished, Marcel took a hunting-rifle and went to explore the neighborhood. Nicaise was fortunate enough to discover a stream of fresh water in a ravine at the base of the mountain, which flowed into the sea. As it was only a short distance away from the place where the *Éclair* was moored, he transported the cooking pots and utensils there in order to prepare a meal.

A fine carpet of grass, enameled by buttercups, appeared to him to be an exquisite table, and he set up the places there without standing on ceremony. Then, joyful and lively, he began to hum his favorite tune. At the same time he built a fire between two stones in order to cook a lobster and a large eel that he had caught earlier under the rocks.

After an hour or so, Marcel came back with two magnificent quail, which made a very good impression on Nicaise. They were immediately put on a spit, and when Trinitus, on his return, perceived the Balthasar's feast that was in preparation, he was momentarily lost for words. The composure of his good friends, however, caused him to burst out laughing. In the shadow of an immense clump of ferns Marcel was placidly opening oysters, and Nicaise, lying on the grass, was methodically turning the wooden spit supporting his roast in front of a bright fire.

Furthermore, while having the part for his thunderbolt manufactured at the smithy, Trinitus had not forgotten that old Nicaise was far from scorning a glass of good wine, and he had brought back two specimens of the finest Azores vintage. The cook declared that it was, indeed, an excellent idea.

They sat on the grass to eat, and chatted for some time about the unfortunate castaways of the *Richmond*. They were more hopeful than ever of finding them one day, and were already promising one another to live as a family in some charming location.

"What joy! What a feast!" said Nicaise. "I feel that I've suddenly woken up as a great chef. After having manned the oar and the spade, I shall finally take up the saucepan. It will be my third transformation."

# CHAPTER FOUR
## THE SECRET WORK
## OF THE WAVES

The shadow of dusk was already bathing the peak of Azores, but the *Éclair*, carefully repaired by Trinitus and his companions, had not yet set forth. The day had been spent fixing under the boat's hull the swings proposed by Marcel, and through one of the tubes that traversed the hull Trinitus had passed the metallic chain and iron harpoon designed, in accordance with Nicaise's wishes, to electrocute the most redoubtable marine animals.

That artificial thunderbolt was a masterpiece of simplicity. On tugging, by means of a rope, a spring attached to the metal rod on which all the electrical currents generated by the piles converged, the rod was put in communication with the upper extremity of the chain that bore the harpoon, and the enormous quantity of electricity expended in moving the boat suddenly became a formidable agent of destruction.

The chain served to conduct the electric fluid into the wound produced by the harpoon in the same way that the string of Franklin's famous kite conducted the lightning stolen from the clouds to the ground.

That terrible weapon, a deadly arrow, was suspended like the sword of Damocles at an equal distance from the three swings, in order that each of them could easily grab it if the need arose. The chain, coiled up like those of the harpoons used on whaling-boats, was about thirty-five meters long. Beside it hung the rope attached to the spring.

It was almost dark when the three voyagers left the Azores. Trinitus immersed the *Éclair* after having drawn away from the numerous reefs that loomed up around the island and took her down to a considerable depth. The manometer tube marked about three hundred meters when the boat resumed its horizontal course.

Around volcanic islands, the extremely uneven sea-bed is bristling with reefs and rocks, imposing and picturesque in form. These masses of stone have flowed from volcanoes in the state of lava; they have been dislocated and overturned by quakes on the Ocean bed, and their volume has gradually increased with the number of submarine eruptions.

When the volcanoes have ceased to produce and heap up these materials, the sea gives them the most various forms, according to its caprice and whim. It has patiently filed, chiseled and sculpted the formless blocks vomited by the craters, completing the work of brute force by means of artistic and almost intelligent toil. Slowly, the crudely-sketched submarine mountains have been refined and dissected; their summits are sharpened into needles and their flanks are pierced through by the continual friction of the waters. Valleys roughly indicated by an obtuse trench have been dug down and hollowed out to very great depths; everywhere, elegance and grace have replaced ponderousness and enormity.

We know how rapidly air, aided by rain and frost, disaggregates the rocks of our mountains. It gives them all kinds of aspects and strange configurations. It is easily understandable that the sea, thanks to the solvent properties of its saline waters, must be far more corrosive than the atmosphere. It bites and gnaws the rocks it bathes incessantly, as the daily degradations of the cliffs of our coasts prove abundantly.

That action of the sea is so powerful that entire islands have sometimes been seen to collapse abruptly into the sea, undermined by the waves. That is how the island of Julia disappeared, in a very short time,[5] and, previously, in 1630 and 1723 two of the small islands in the Azores archipelago.

Thus, when Trinitus and his companions, clad in their diving suits and placidly seated on their swings, found themselves more than three hundred meters below the surface of the waves, they perceived with great astonishment that they had descended into a veritable submarine palace.

The innumerable reefs through which they were

---

5. The volcanic island named Julia by the French emerged off the coat of Sicily in July 1831. The British called it Graham Island and the Spanish Ferdinandea. Britain, France, and Italy came to the brink of armed conflict in their determination to claim the new island, but the problem resolved itself when the island sank again after a matter of months.

prudently steering a path, slowing the progress of the *Éclair* as much as possible, seemed to them to be the debris of a multitude of fantastic monuments rather than rocks. They might have thought that they were looking at the majestic ruins of an immense city. Pillars, columns and porticoes of a prodigious height loomed up around the boat. Audacious buttresses protruded and overlapped on all sides; bottomless caves and grottoes displayed their monstrous orifices here and there; balustrades and open galleries crowned enormous masses that the water had not been able to fashion.

On the sea-bed, at the level of the ground supporting all that magical architecture, extremely narrow streets opened, enormous crevices, fissures and gaps of incredible depth.

Suddenly, however, the three fearful voyagers saw a porch of enormous dimensions yawning in from of them like the gate of Hell. The Ocean was engulfed in pitch darkness under the mysterious vaults that continues it.

Amazed, Trinitus put the boat into reverse.

In the presence of that gigantic portal, which opened to an immeasurable abyss, Nicaise and Marcel were similarly nonplussed. Where did that immense submarine tunnel lead? Was it prudent to go into it? Might it not be a labyrinth from which they would not be able to get out? Those were the grave questions that the voyagers asked themselves. The splendor of the landscape unfurling around the boat caused them to regard the gulf full of darkness with dire suspicion. It seemed to them that they were about to quit the domain of life in order to enter that of death.

Truly, they had before their eyes a striking antithesis. Everywhere, on the rocks through which they had just made their way, a magnificent vegetation rose up. The sea, after having made the lava it submerged into an extraordinary city, had populated it with millions of animals and plants. The porticos, columns, pillars and buttresses were coated with living beings, which masked the cracks and protrusions of the rock. The stone disappeared beneath that magical flowering. Legions of fish were traveling through the arches; groups of zoophytes and polyps raised up their animated branches on every side; myriads of medusas hung from the vaults of grottoes like chandeliers abundantly laden with crystals. All these marvels were immersed in the calm and profound azure of the Ocean.

By contrast, ahead of Trinitus' boat opened a somber cavern that seemed to have been hollowed out to shelter the most frightful monsters. The sea must be hiding therein all the deformities that it dared not display in the light; even the opening of the gulf, as menacing as the maw of a hyena, seemed to be constricted by a frightful rictus. It had a repulsive and hideous expression.

At that sight, Trinitus consulted his companions.

"Ought we to go in?" he asked.

"What if we veer to starboard?" asked Nicaise.

"That's possible, but then we'll hurl ourselves into the Sargasso Sea, where the algae will hinder our passage. This tunnel will probably take us in the direction of the Canaries, which would suit us very well...."

"Well," said Marcel, "let's try to go in."

"What do you think, Nicaise?" asked Trinitus.

"Me? If you're not afraid, I'm not afraid!"

"You're a brave man! Forwards, then!" said Trinitus.

The *Éclair* resumed its progress and plunged into the abyss. The width of the tunnel was considerable; the boat's lamp, illuminating the liquid mass that filled the gulf, only cast a vague light on to its walls. A few *Actinia* and cephalopods could, however, be made out there, on ledges in the rock. Crabs and sea-urchins were crawling along the bottom. In the somber retreats of the vault, indefinable creatures were stirring confusedly.

No obstacle impeded the progress of the *Éclair*, and Trinitus thought that he could increase her speed without danger. The boat moved rapidly, and the voyagers soon consolidated the hope that they would find the Canary Isles at the far end of the tunnel.

Suddenly, the prow of the vessel collided violently with the rock, and the *Éclair* leapt backwards.

That recoil, determined by the ingenious apparatus Trinitus had invented, preserved the boat from certain ruin. It was the end of the tunnel; there was reason to fear that it terminated in a cul-de-sac.

Trinitus, seeing the boat's path closed in all directions, looked up, and perceived that the vault of the tunnel was lacking at this location. Having been horizontal, the submarine tunnel had become vertical, rising up perpendicularly.

The scientist changed direction, and the vessel rose up like a balloon into the gulf, whose direction encouraged the presumption that it would open at the surface of the sea. The voyagers were hoisted up the enormous stone tube as if they were being raised from the bottom of a well. Suddenly, however, after a long ascent, the *Éclair* came to an abrupt halt. She had emerged into an immense grotto hollowed out under a mountain, the only exit from which was the submarine tunnel that the *Éclair* had just traversed.

Trinitus and his companions disembarked on to dry land. They lit torches and climbed a rocky hill that loomed up in front of them. When they reached the summit, however, they uttered a cry of fright. Another gulf more than a hundred meters in diameter opened before their feet. They lay down on their stomachs in order to gaze into that abyss, and Trinitus threw his torch into it in order to illuminate it. Its side walls were bathed in a red glow, and then it suddenly went out—but it was only some time afterwards that they heard it hit the ground.

Trinitus reflected momentarily.

"This abyss is six hundred meters deep," he said. "It can only be the chimney of the great volcano of Tenerife, and the tunnel we've just followed must be one of its submarine ramifications."

# CHAPTER FIVE
## THE CHIMNEY OF TENERIFE

The intelligent captain of the *Éclair* was not mistaken when he assured his frightened companions that they had emerged into the chimney of Tenerife. The bold voyagers had indeed traversed the flanks of the great volcano of the Canaries. The interior orifice of the tunnel opened like a window into that immense well filled with thick vapors and sulfurous gases. The unbreathable atmosphere extinguished torches, and the reckless explorers would inevitably have been asphyxiated is they had not received a continuous supply of the boat's artificial air through their respiratory tubes.

Below the rock on which they were sitting, the abyss uttered dull rumbles from time to time. It seemed that a monster of unimaginable proportions was coughing in the depths of that cyclopean dungeon; it was both the cry of rage and the plaint of Enceladus crushed beneath Etna.

Those heart-rending sighs terrified Nicaise and Marcel. Only Trinitus interrogated the gulf avidly, seeking to understand the hoarse and formidable voice rising up to him. His ears were open to all sounds, and his curious gaze searched the darkness; in his excited brain, a thousand problems found their solution. The scientist had completely blotted out the mariner.

The volcanic chimney extended above the enormous opening of the tunnel, on its way to opening into the atmosphere in a vast crater. Trinitus looked up continually to see whether daylight might be visible through the orifice of the volcano, but he could not discern the slightest gleam of sunlight.

"It's very strange," he said, "that a crater some four hundred and fifty meters in diameter doesn't allow us to glimpse the sky. It's true that the crater opens at three thousand seven hundred meters above our heads—a distance that must shrink it considerably from our point of view.…"

"Doctor," said Marcel, "I think it's time to go. Listen to that terrible rumbling!"

"The thousand million devils of Hell must have fallen into that hole!" Nicaise added. "Let's get out of here, I beg you."

"Poltroons!" said Trinitus. "We're in the presence of a spectacle that we might be the first ever to contemplate."

"We can't see anything," Marcel replied. "Our torches have gone out."

"That's the effect of carbon dioxide and sulfur dioxide," the scientist replied.

"But you expect to receive light from above?" asked Nicaise.

"I hoped so, at first, but now I understand why that

isn't the case. Tenerife is an extinct volcano, but its crater still emits smoke. The chimney, and, in consequence, the peak it occupies, rises three thousand seven hundred meters above sea level. At present, we're at sea level; between our eyes and the crater, therefore, we have a column of smoke three thousand seven hundred meters thick, which must be impenetrable to rays of sunlight.

Marcel was about to reply to Trinitus when a loud explosion suddenly resounded at the bottom of the abyss. A red light suddenly illuminated the interior of the volcano. The walls of the gulf, bristling with gigantic blocks of rock, sparkled like ardent coals. A torrent of thick vapors and incandescent ashes rose up rapidly in the enormous chimney, which resembled a brazier.

Dazzled by the instantaneous blaze, the three companions were struck by terror and amazement. Even Trinitus shivered, thinking that his last hour had come.

A colossal plateau of ardent lava was seething at their feet. That ocean of molten rock had invaded the chimney of the volcano and was rising toward the voyagers with a terrifying rapidity. It was the beginning of an eruption.

In a few seconds, that frightful tide of liquefied minerals would reach the rock on which Trinitus and his companions were positioned. It would reach the opening of the tunnel and gush with a tremendous racket into the submarine gallery.

The three men, petrified by the sight of the mountain of fire that was rising up from the depths of the inferno to swallow them, clung on to the rock, with no thought of taking flight. They felt already calcined by that flamboyant mass, which was melting the very walls of the volcano as it covered them. Frightful crackling sounds were audible; that was the rocks and sides of the volcanic chimney cracking on contact with the horrible furnace. Attempting to escape its reach seemed absurd to Trinitus, and to his companions, so with haggard eyes and their hair bristling in fear, they waited for their final moment.

The lava was still rising.

Suddenly, however, after a formidable crack, there was a shrill whistle. The chimney had burst at the level of the submarine tunnel, and a stream of water was falling into the furnace through a narrow fissure.

That strident whistle extracted Trinitus from his stupor. He grabbed Nicaise with one hand and Marcel with the other.

"Let's go!" he cried. "Perhaps the *Éclair* will have time to get out of the tunnel before the lava reaches this level.…"

But Nicaise and Marcel, already gripped by the vertigo of the abyss, did not understand that Trinitus, at that supreme moment, was still thinking of salvation. They looked at the scientist in bewilderment, and remained nailed to the spot in spite of his supplications, on the burning rock that was gradually bursting and splintering underfoot. Fear had rendered them foolish.

Meanwhile, the roaring of the gulf was growing louder, and the ardent lava was still rising.

"Come on! Come on!" cried Trinitus. "We still have time!"

"We're doomed!" said Nicaise.

"It's too late!" murmured Marcel.

"I beg you…follow me!" implored the scientist, devoured by the cruelest anguish. "The *Éclair* goes so quickly! We can save ourselves!"

It was in vain. Trinitus' two friends, paralyzed by fear and overwhelmed by the very horror of the death that threatened them, remained motionless, resistant to the scientist's efforts. The death they had glimpsed was so grandiose and imposing that instead of trying to avoid it, they were impelled to move toward it.

"Oh, my God!" the unfortunate Trinitus continued to shout. "Here comes the lava! It's going to spread over us! Come on, for Heaven's sake!"

The immense lake of fire rose higher and higher, as if driven by some infernal power. Sprays of flame and torrents of vapor escaped from its bosom; immense bubbles burst on its surface with explosions as resounding as cannon fire, making the mass of molten minerals seethe, like an ocean whipped up by a tempest.

The innumerable echoes of the volcanic chimney were repeating the rumbles and explosions of lava, and the entire volcano was shivering like a sick person tormented by fever.

Suddenly, the portion of rock on which Nicaise

and Marcel were still standing broke away abruptly and fell into the gulf with a noise like that of thunder. The rupture took place almost under the feet of the voyagers, and all three uttered screams of terror and despair, thinking that they were about to be hurled into the abyss.

That violent shock revived the instinct of survival in Nicaise and Marcel. Dragged away by one last effort from Trinitus, they made an abrupt backward movement, and tumbled with the scientist to the foot of the slope that they had climbed on quitting the boat.

The *Éclair* was there, ready to receive them, but it was impossible to get in via the cylinder established underneath the hull. The proximity of the lava had raised the temperature of the water in the submarine tunnel by about sixty degrees.

This time, Trinitus understood that it was impossible to escape death. However, he detached the respiratory tube from his diving apparatus, and made his companions do the same. Breathless, and prey to the greatest anxiety, they hastily opened one of the boat's portholes. Nicaise and Marcel hurled themselves into the cabin, and the scientist threw himself after them, after closing the door behind him.

He was just in time!

At that moment, in fact, the debris of the rock separating the *Éclair* from the volcanic chimney collapsed in a whirlwind of incandescent scoria, and the voyagers, half-dead, saw a broad stripe of fire reach the enormous breach that had just opened up.

It was boiling lava, ready to overflow into the tunnel.

"Here it comes!" cried Marcel.

"It's all over! Commend your soul to God," sighed Nicaise.

But Trinitus had seized the lever that caused the electric current to flow into the boat's engine, and the *Éclair* was suddenly engulfed in the water of the tunnel, the temperature of which was still rising. The wall separating them from the volcanic chimney was probably vitrified by then by contact with the lava, and in the boat's cabin the heat was so intense that Trinitus was expecting further misfortunes at any moment.

What the scientist feared most was, however, on the contrary, what saved him and his companions. In fact, the electric piles—whose power, as everyone knows, increases with temperature—greatly stimulated by the heat of the water in the tunnel, redoubled their activity and promptly furnished the *Éclair* with enough electricity to double her speed.

In a matter of seconds, the tunnel was traversed, and Trinitus' boat emerged, pell-mell, with a vat number of cephalopods, medusas, *Actinia*, crustaceans, conger eels, sharks and other marine animals fleeing the imminent catastrophe.

Suddenly, a horrible noise, which could only be compared with the simultaneous discharge of several artillery batteries, resounded under the sea.

"It's the lava irrupting into the tunnel!" Trinitus exclaimed. "But we're out of reach now!"

Marcel and Nicaise, moved to tears, threw their

arms around the scientist.

That day, the inhabitants of Tenerife, after a few earth tremors, perceived that the volcano was vomiting thick clouds of water vapor. The eruption had no other consequences; the submarine tunnel, filled by lava, might well have preserved the island from a catastrophe.

# CHAPTER SIX
## THE SARGASSO SEA

After having escaped the terrible danger they had run in the tunnel, Trinitus and his two friends found themselves in the presence of the mysterious Sargasso Sea, into which the captain of the *Éclair* had not dared to venture. It was, however, necessary now to resolve to do so, for navigation under the waves was impossible along the coast of Africa because of the innumerable reefs strewn along the route, and the sea was so rough that day that it would have been very dangerous to travel near the surface.

Trinitus made his companions party to his perplexity. "My dear friends," he said, "the safest route that we can follow now is precisely the one we wanted to avoid. We're going to traverse the Sargasso Sea to reach the Cape Verde Islands."

"Hmmm!" said Nicaise, shaking his head. "We'll never get out of it!"

"Get away!" said Marcel. "The Doctor's just saved us from the Inferno—he can't lose us in a submarine forest."

The old mariner shrugged his shoulders. "You're

talking like a child," he told his nephew. "If you knew the Sargasso, you'd talk differently, I can assure you...."

"It's just seaweed!"

"Yes, seaweeds no less than a thousand meters long. The *Éclair* will cut a fine figure in that salad: an eel in a haycart."

"Plants a kilometer long! Is that possible?" asked Marcel.

"Perfectly," Trinitus replied. "Nicaise is right. The Sargasso kelps, which mariners call 'tropical vines' because they bear berries similar to grapes, reach vast lengths in this reason. Naturalists call the algae 'floating fucus' and in the sea we have to traverse they're so thick and numerous that their interlaced branches sometimes halt the progress of ships."

"I didn't know that," Marcel said, but added: "Is the Sargasso Sea very extensive?"

"It has four or five times the surface area of France," Trinitus replied. "It occupies all the space between the Azores, the Canaries, the Cape Verde Islands and the fiftieth degree of longitude."

"That's scarcely reassuring," Marcel went on, "but in the end, since we have no choice, it's necessary to go that way."

"It's better, in fact," Trinitus continued, "to be hampered by long grass than broken by rocks...."

"That's very true," muttered Nicaise, "but I'm curious to know how we'll get out of it."

"With courage!" Marcel replied.

Trinitus took the helm, and the *Éclair* set off in the

direction of the Cape Verde Islands.

"How is it," Nicaise's nephew asked, all of a sudden, "that all these algae that form the Sargasso Sea are gathered in such great number in the same place?"

"Nothing is more natural," Trinitus replied, "but in order to understand the phenomenon, one has to have an idea of the countless currents that circulate in the Ocean. It's necessary to know that in the immense seas that bathe three-quarters of the globe, there isn't a drop of water that isn't incessantly in movement. These liquid masses, which some people think are only whipped up by the winds, labor almost intelligently. They're agitated and stirred by currents of two types; some circulate vertically, from the surface to the sea-bed, other horizontally, from one point on the surface to another, or at various depths.

"The sun, the salt contained in the sea water and the polyps that coat the submarine rocks with their accretions are the sole agents of the regular and continuous movements accomplished in the bosom of the oceans.

"In the tropics, the sun rapidly evaporates the superficial layer of sea water. That water, as it evaporates, abandons its salt to the layers immediately beneath, the weight of which is considerably increased. They tend to descend toward the sea-bed, and, in consequence, establish a vertically descendant current.

On the sea-bed, however live innumerable legions of polyps, and those animals work in the opposite direction to the sun. They diminish the density of the profound layers of water that bathe them, by depriving them of their salts to build their concretions, and those aqueous layers, made lighter, rise up toward the surface, establishing a vertically ascendant current."

"My word," said Marcel, "that does indeed make two vertical currents, one determined by the heat of the sun, descending toward the sea-bed, and the other determined by the polyps, rising up from the bottom of the sea toward the surface."

"That's right," said Trinitus. "Now let's get back to the tropics. Evaporation tend to lower the level of the sea there, but the winds drive all the water vapor that rises into the atmosphere toward the pole. In the polar regions, the aqueous vapors condense into clouds, which fall as torrential rain, and in those regions the sea-level rises to the same extent that it falls in the tropics."

"What rises up falls down again...that's quite natural," Nicaise put in.

"However," the scientist continued, "that difference in level being unable to exist because of the mobility of the liquid, two great currents are established between the pole and the equator, and between the equator and the pole, in order to reestablish the disrupted equilibrium. The former are currents of cold water, the latter currents of warm water, and it's the most remarkable of them, the Gulf Stream, that maintains the Sargasso Sea in the area that it occupies.

"The Gulf Stream is the largest current of warm water that we know. It is born in the Gulf of Mexico, escapes via the Bahama Channel along the coast of

North America as far as the banks of Newfoundland, and from there travels eastwards as far as the Azores. There it divides into two branches; one follows the African coast, only departing therefrom at the Equator to be confused with the great equatorial current; the other goes into the Channel and the North Sea to die away in the Arctic Ocean.

"The velocity of the Gulf Stream is equal to that of our most rapid rivers, but the mass of water that it carries is two or three thousand times greater than that of the largest watercourse irrigating the land.

"That immense current traverses the Atlantic with such impetuosity that its waters don't mingle with those of the Ocean. Their deep blue color—due to the large quantity of salt they carry—cuts cleanly through the greenish waters that form the mobile banks of the majestic stream.

"In the polar regions, the temperature of the Gulf Stream, even in winter, is several degrees above that of the glacial seas traversed by the current. So, on contact with those warm waters, the northern countries bathed by the Arctic Ocean feel their ice melting and the rigor of their climate mollified. The Gulf Stream warms the desolate lands of the pole; it carries the equatorial sun to them, dissolved, so to speak, in its azure waves, and brings them enough warmth from the tropical regions for them to extract a measure of spring therefrom. The vast Atlantic current is the great artery of the Ocean. Its warm waters spread life in the countries disinherited by the sun, as arterial blood distributes it to our organs.

"If you examine the southern branch of the Gulf Stream on a map, you'll see that, by joining up with the great equatorial current, it forms an almost complete ring around the Sargasso Sea. It's therefore natural that an immense mass of marine plants should occupy the center of the ring in question, the Gulf Stream behaving in regard to the weeds as a whirlpool does with regard to the floating objects that it surrounds with its moving girdle."

While Trinitus was speaking, Nicaise and Marcel listened in silence to the lesson in physical geography. In a magnificent atlas open on the table, the scientist showed them the direction of all the oceanic currents. That study appeared to be very interesting to the old mariner, who had not thought the sea capable of such great things. He had only ever heard mention of currents in a very incomplete fashion; he was quite ignorant of the salutary influence of their warm waters, and imagined that Nature, in placing them in the bosom of her seas, had had no other objective than setting traps for vessels in order to drive them off course and get them lost.

Trinitus enabled him to understand that, thanks to the work of Franklin and Humboldt and, especially, the recent endeavors of Commandant Maury, currents were, on the contrary, highways, which it was very important to know, and of which navigators ought to be able to take advantage, in order to accelerate the speed of their vessels.

After that lesson on the circulation of the Ocean, Nicaise felt full of admiration. The sea, which he had always regarded as a terrible and brutal mass, suddenly seemed to him to be benevolent and intelligent. Those transparent waves he could see through the windows of the *Éclair* seemed to him to be full of life; in his enthusiasm, he compared the vertical and horizontal currents to the veins and arteries of his own body— but what charmed him most was the simplicity of the causes which put that powerful force, the Ocean, in movement. Up above, a ray of sunlight and a gust of wind; down below, a feeble animalcule, the polyp; in the water, a few more-or-less numerous parcels of a simple mineral, salt—and that was sufficient to stir the seas from top to bottom!

In those immeasurable abysses, not a single drop of water was useless; the most humble liquid molecule had its role and its task. Sometimes it furnished materials to the polyps; sometimes it rose up as vapor to fall back as rain; sometimes cold and deprived, it ran from the pole to the equator; sometimes, warm and vivifying, having been regenerated by the sun, it raced from the equator to the pole to warm up the icy extremities of the aging globe.

Marcel had listened no less attentively to Trinitus' explanations. The imposing grandeur and admirable harmony of nature struck him with astonishment.

Suddenly, immense walls of fantastic vegetables loomed up around the *Éclair*, but she, traveling at top speed, sheared through them as it passed by, like a scythe through wheat-stalks.

Soon, however, enlaced by thousands of green cords, the boat came to a halt.

She was on the edge of the Sargasso Sea.

# CHAPTER SEVEN
## THE HERD OF SPERM WHALES

As soon as the *Éclair* had plunged into the kelp thickets of the Sargasso Sea, Trinitus understood, by virtue of the resistance that boat was experiencing, how long and difficult the crossing would be.

"I can only see one thing to do," he said to his companions. "We have to go down on to the swings, attach ourselves solidly, in order not to be pulled off by the marine plants that might get a grip on us, and clear a path for *Éclair* with the aid of our harpoons when the algae prevent it from moving forward."

"Aha!" said Marcel. "My swings are going to render us a valuable service!"

"They're going to save us," Trinitus replied, hastily donning his diving-suit.

"Patience!" observed the prudent Nicaise. "We can't take too many precautions. The sea we're about to traverse is a veritable virgin forest. We'll find an infinity of marine animals there, which we might be forced to fight. Let's not forget our knives."

"You're right," Trinitus replied. "We ought to be ready or any eventuality. Let's arm ourselves from head to toe, and let's remember, in order not to lose courage, that we have an electric thunderbolt capable of killing our most enormous enemies."

Having concluded his preparations, the scientist slipped through the large cylinder that opened under the boat, connected up the glazed helmet of his apparatus to the rubber tube that drew air from the cabin, and sat down on one of the three swings.

Nicaise and Marcel did not take long to join him, and, the long weeds that had wrapped themselves around the *Éclair* having been cut or torn away by the barbs of harpoons, the vessel, although continually hampered by gigantic vegetation, was nevertheless able to continue on its way.

The algae became gradually denser, however; they were so thick and tangled that, as Christopher Columbus had expressed it, "the sea seemed imprisoned, as if by ice." The waters, transformed into a kind of green magma, seemed to be solidifying. This region of the Ocean could no longer be compared to anything but a submerged forest, and Trinitus' boat was entangled by those avalanches of foliage like an ant in a bale of straw.

Immense vegetal curtains formed oscillating partitions in front of her, through which it was necessary to clear a path like a circus performer bursting through paper hoops. The work was hard, though, and eventually became impossible. The three voyagers became extremely weary. cutting, parting and tearing away the thousand verdant arms that seized and shackled them in their course.

Furthermore, they had to defend themselves against the redoubtable fish and mollusks that swarmed in the sea. With thrusts of the harpoon they drove away walruses, sharks, moray eels and dogfish, and were obliged on two occasions to make use of the electric thunderbolt to kill giant octopodes that extended their horrible tentacles toward them.

When the impenetrable forest cleared slightly, however, the most grandiose and magical spectacle was offered to their gaze. Marcel and Nicaise were amazed and Trinitus dazzled by what they saw.

In addition to the immense quantity of kelp fronds laden with their clusters of fruits, all the known kinds of algae were flourishing around them, and the scientist discovered a good many that had never figured in any botanist's herbarium.

From the midst of thick bushes of *Laminaria* and flat-leaved *Colaconema* projected cyclindrical *Lomentaria*, covered with hyaline mucilage, like a coating of crystal. The broad fronds of the *Chondrus* were like rich curtains that looked as if they were capriciously cut out in pink taffeta. The *Amansia* deployed their lacy networks with prodigious luxury, and the *Claudea* their serpentine membranous extensions. Through that heaped-up mass crawled the unctuous cylinders of the intestinal *Ulva*, which mariners call sea-guts. *Catenella* and *Choetophora*, which resemble long rosaries with enormous beads, fell in garlands over the embroideries of *Anadyomenes* and *Chordaria*, enlacing their nacreous cartilaginous threads with sheaves of *Fucus*, over which thousands of *Acetabularia* opened their elegant parasols.

But those profound masses of vegetables of every color harbored myriads of animals, the most humble of which were feeding on the algae while the larger hones hunted the smaller. All kinds of mollusks could be seen there, all kind of crustacean and all possible zoophytes. Briliantly colored shellfish—porcelains, buccinas, *Patellas*, *Neritinas*, murexes, *Haliotis*, and so on—hung like fruits from the extremities of the plants, and through the azure water that bathed that fantastic society passed legions of crabs, *Palemons*, *Nemertes* and *Syllis* with innumerable rings, *Apolemias* and *Prayas*, like animate fringes trailing sparkling networks in the bosom of the waves.

After two hours of hard labor to expose all these marvels, however, the three companions felt their strength giving out. The envisaged themselves, with terror, trapped in the middle of the Sargasso Sea, and Trinitus, prey to dolorous apprehensions, found himself extremely embarrassed, perhaps for the first time in his life.

Having expended all their courage and all their strength in impotent efforts and mighty struggles, the scientist and his fearful companions recognized the horror of their situation.

The boat had been caught in a tangle of long marine algae, as if in the toils of a gigantic net, and all the attempts they made to extract it from the horrible grip of those viscous lianas only served to entangle it further. It was attached, bound and enchained to the sea-bed, and, as if by a cruel irony, those inextricable chains were garlands of flowers.

The captive *Éclair* had struggled and resisted in vain, but it had fallen prey to living creatures that were hanging on to every part of it. It was agonizing in the knots of verdure that clutched it, as a fly trapped in a spider's web is strangled by the silky threads with which the monster enlaces it. All those strange vegetables seemed to be retaining it with a sort of savage pleasure, and thousands of marine animals were gathering around its metallic hull, which seemed to be exciting their curiosity to the highest degree. The fish were sniffing it with astonishment; the surprised crustaceans were palpating and caressing it with their antennas; the sticky mollusks were crawling insolently over it; the polyps and sponges were attaching their large feet to it and boldly taking possession of it.

Gradually, the copper dome disappeared under a cloak of algae and marine monsters.

The ropes and swings, and the voyagers themselves, were not treated with any more respect. Flora and fauna as terrible as they were picturesque invaded them. Hideous legions of crabs took hold of them; a host of anemones and medusas fixed themselves to the diving apparatus, and, like Philemon and Baucis, the unfortunate navigators seemed to have been transformed into vegetables. But that burial of three men under organic beings full of life was frightful. Trinitus foresaw the moment when numbers would triumph over strength and dexterity, and the specter of the most horrible death loomed up in his imagination.

All those hideous mouths were agape around the *Éclair*, impotent henceforth to flee them. All those maws with sharp teeth, all those pincers, all those grippers, all those suckers, all those hooks, all those talons and all those claws, the number of which was increasing incessantly, were destined to tear the poor scientist and his unfortunate companions into a thousand pieces.

How could they escape that frightful death, those atrocious tortures, that horrible agony? No one could think of it; any salvation seemed impossible—and they were all too frightened to murmur or complain.

Go back into the boat? That was evidently the only means of escaping imminent death—but then it would be necessary to resign themselves to remain trapped in the algae and wait for death by starvation, a hundred times more frightful than the one that presented itself immediately.

Without making his friends party to the cruel anguish to which he was prey, Trinitus nevertheless decided that it was necessary to go back into the ship right away, if only to see what remained to be done in such a grave circumstance. Marcel and Nicaise went into the cabin first; Trinitus slid in behind them and all three took off the glazed helmets of their apparatus. Their bleak expressions bore the imprint of fatigue and despair, but no tears were shining in their eyes. They had made their decision!

While Nicaise and Marcel sat down on the floor leaning their heads against the wall, however, Trinitus still faithful to science, armed himself with his instruments in order to calculate the distance that separated them from the Cape Verde Islands.

"Twenty-third degree of latitude!" he exclaimed.

"I didn't think I'd die there," Nicaise replied, coldly, in a reproachful tone.

But the scientist had picked up a pen and was writing in a notebook: *In this area the Sargasso Sea is thicker than anywhere else. The algae here are inextricable and thousands of marine animals swarm here....*

Suddenly, a cry of amazement and fright uttered by Marcel made the scientist shudder and extracted Nicaise from his sad thoughts.

"Listen! Listen!" shouted the young man.

A dull and prolonged rumble, like distant thunder, was audible a long way away under the waves.

Trinitus paled frightfully, and Nicaise's eyes lit up.

"They're whales!" stammered the scientist.

The rumble was replicated, nearer and more distinctly.

"They're following the same route that we've traveled and coming straight toward us," he added.

The roar was heard again, formidable and profound this time, like the noise of two hundred organs resonating at the same time.

Nicaise and Marcel uttered a terrible cry. "We're doomed!" Although they were leaning on one another, they feel to their knees.

Trinitus' face became suddenly radiant, however, and the scientist seized the tiller with both hands. "Saved!" he cried. "We're saved!"

Immediately, in the midst of a frightful din and upheaval, the *Éclair* was abruptly snatched out of her prison, as if she were being dragged away by some frightful avalanche, or lifted up—like a feather, so to speak—by an irresistible force.

Three or four frightful shocks caused Nicaise and Marcel to sprawl on the floor, half-dead with fright, but Trinitus, having foreseen everything, had clung on to the vessel's wall with on hand, and was still gripping the tiller with the other.

The formidable animals that had rushed upon the *Éclair* in this manner were enormous sperm whales, which traverse the Sargasso Sea in tightly-knit groups. Hazard had determined that Trinitus' boat should be in their way, and they had impetuously pushed it before them, without any suspicion of the service they were rendering to the scientist and his companions.

Trinitus had understood that these gigantic animals would have no difficulty in clearing a path through the middle of the algae and the idea had suddenly occurred to him of taking advantage of it. So, when the irresistible column, composed of at least fifty individuals, had passed by, the scientist bravely launched the *Éclair* in pursuit of them, sticking as close as he could to the charming monsters that were clearing a way for him. His face animated, his eyes shining and his hair bristling, Trinitus did not spare his joy.

"Come on, Nicaise! Marcel!" he cried. "Get up! We're flying like the wind! We're on the heels of the sperm whales—and what tugs they are. Damn, that's fast! They're taking us straight toward the Cape Verde Islands. It's charming! No hindrance! Not one alga— they're clearing them all away as they pass. Forward ho!"

And while his stupefied companions seemed to be emerging from a dream, the scientist, magnificent in his boldness, stimulated and drove his boat, as if she were some kind of marine monster submissive to his voice and docile to his magical power.

By the silvery light of the electric lamp, Trinitus, clad in his diving-suit, streaming and laden with focus, polyps and anemones, resembled the god of the Oceans. As if he were riding in triumph, he followed the gigantic cetaceans that were clearing the route for him. Legions of dolphins, walruses, seals and porpoises launched themselves in his wake; the roars of the sperm whales resounded, sowing fear in front of him; shreds of crushed and broken kelp were floating in all directions. No marine divinity had such a cortege in his Estates, no Amphitrite or Neptune, sailing on a nacreous shell, had ever been escorted as Trinitus was.

The sperm whales were traveling at an average of sixteen kilometers an hour in spite of the obstacles they encountered in the overgrown sea. Just as a herd of wild boar tracked by hunters opens a way through the most impenetrable thickets, the enormous cetaceans, most of which were twenty meters in length, cut through the middle of the kelp that was in their path. One of them had bumped its head on Trinitus' boat, and it was to that formidable impact that the *Éclair* owed its salvation.

Following a habit particular to the animals in question, which several naturalists have observed, a leader was swimming at the head of the column and directing it. It is probable that it was leading its companions to the austral seas, doubtless populated at the present time by emigrant fish to which the sperm whales would give chase.

That leader must, moreover, have been an excellent guide, for Trinitus recognized, by means of his compass, that it was following the most direct route with a much precision as the most experienced pilot could have done.

The scientist was not unaware, however, that these sperm whale captains are sometimes incapable of fulfilling these high functions, so he remained on guard. He was well aware that one day, thirty-two sperm whales guided by an inexpert leader had run aground on the beach of Audierne Bay in Finistère, and he was familiar with many other examples of the same kind.

Furthermore, Nicaise, having recovered almost completely, and after having congratulated Trinitus on his composure, began to tell a string of stories about the cetaceans whose tracks the *Éclair* was following. He gave the still-tremulous Marcel a hoist of details regarding their habits, and his heart was full of gratitude for the monsters that he had once gone to combat in the Northern seas with fishermen from Calais and Boulogne. He explained how the unfortunate animals were harpooned and how their skulls were opened in order to collect the greasy white substance known in the arts by the name of spermaceti. It was a natural history lesson to which Trinitus and Marcel listened with great interest—but the old mariner swore, by way of conclusion, that he would never again take up arms against sperm whales.

Meanwhile, the kelp gradually thinned out and the cetaceans were swimming with fearful speed.

Trinitus determined the latitude again, and had the pleasure of announcing to his companions that they were scarcely six leagues away from the Cape Verde Islands.

# CHAPTER EIGHT
## FROM CAPE VERDE TO
## THE CAPE OF GOOD HOPE

It was only when they were level with the initial islets of the archipelago that Trinitus resolved to quit the trail of the sperm whales, to which he was exceedingly grateful. The monstrous cetaceans, still guided by their captain, turned abruptly south-westwards off the cape of Santa Antão, and the scientist piloting the *Éclair*, after have wished his liberators bon voyage, took his boat into the narrow strait separating the islands of Sal and São Nicolau.

To begin with he followed a kind of volcanic alleyway, a submarine crevice of extreme depth, and emerged from it a few minutes later, fearing that the *Éclair* might run into a reef, opposite the old town of Santiago, the largest in the Cape Verde archipelago.

Two rocks, rising ten or twelve meters out of the water and almost contiguous, formed a kind of comprehensively-sheltered little bay, into which Trinitus steered in order to moor the boat and disembark with his two companions.

At the base of the overlapping rocks, vesicular fucus

grew in dense clumps, along with veritable meadows of *Zostera*, and on the narrow platform they presented, a few grasses, beaten by the winds, were vegetating in the cracks in the stone.

As the travelers approached, the seagulls that inhabited the sterile islets flew away in alarm, but the cunning Nicaise took advantage of their departure to search their nests, and brought back half a dozen eggs, which he proposed to cook for the evening meal.

Meanwhile, Marcel had climbed the rock and, standing on the platform, contemplated delightedly the magnificent panorama that was unfurled around him. Trinitus and Nicaise, excited by his cries of admiration, climbed up to the summit of the reef in their turn, and all three, profoundly moved by the sublime spectacle that they had before their eyes, thanked the Providence that had miraculously brought them this far.

The Ocean, calm and transparent, lay before them all the way to Santiago, whose principal town they could see on the horizon, sited on the edge of the waves. A few fishing-boats, their sails inflated by the wind, were coming out of the harbor, vividly illuminated by the ardent sun, swaying gracefully on the blue waters of the Atlantic. The seagulls, in their bold flight, brushed the crests of the waves uttering joyful cries; and from time to time, a fish, leaping out of the water, darted silvery reflections in the sunlight.

Beyond the town of Santiago were the island's mountains, whose volcanic peaks, like those of the Azores and Canaries, were lost in the azure of the sky.

The mildness and beauty of the landscape made Marcel sigh and filled Trinitus' soul with melancholy. They were both thinking about the cherished individuals for whom they were undertaking this perilous voyage. Trinitus wondered whether God would permit him ever to see his beloved wife and daughter again, Marcel whether he would ever hold hands with his tender fiancée Alice.

To these moving question posed by their hearts, they dared not make any reply. They saw in their imagination, on one side misfortune, the most horrible death, the most frightful catastrophe that it was possible to conceive, and on the other, joy, happiness, the most perfect felicity that one could experience in this world.

Which was the truth? They were both impatient to find out and fearful. Marcel, especially since he had escaped a death that he had believed to be inevitable in the heart of the Sargasso Sea, was hopeful and inclined toward happiness. Trinitus, his brow anxious, as if he could still see a yawning gulf full of darkness at his feet, could hardly make any but sad assumptions.

As for Nicaise, insouciant but grumpy, like a mariner who has sailed all the seas, thought through the smoke of his pipe that with all the spermaceti that could have been collected from the skulls of the sperm whales to which they owed their lives, they could have secured an income of at least sixty thousand francs a year. He estimated that those "diabolical animals," collectively, were carrying two million in merchandise Now that the old mariner was out of danger, that was the form that his gratitude took.

Suddenly, Trinitus broke the silence that had reigned for some time. "My dear friends," he said, "after the terrible dangers we've run, who can tell what Providence still has in store for us? In order to arrive in the midst of these Oceanic islands, we've only covered a quarter of the distance that still remains for us to travel. Before going any further, reflect. If you're hesitant about following me, I can leave you in Santiago. To return to France, you can take one of the steamships that come from the Cape or the River Plate once a week, and I'll depart alone for Australia...."

At these words, the indignant Nicaise straightened up so precipitately that he broke three of the eggs he had collected. That ill-timed omelet raised his fury to the point of paroxysm.

"Damnation!" he said. "Rather than do that, I'd prefer to be chewed like a plug of tobacco by all the sharks in the world!"

As for Marcel, he contented himself with squeezing Trinitus' hand gently.

Five minutes later, the *Éclair*, carrying the three companions, disappeared under the waves again.

On leaving Cape Verde, Trinitus steered his boat toward Ascension Island, which, like its neighbor Saint Helena, is nothing but an enormous basaltic rock rearing up in the middle of the ocean.

The scientist promised himself firmly not to stop there, for he was burning with desire to reach the Cape of Good Hope, and, thanks to the *Éclair*'s speed, he was not expecting to take two days to arrive there.

It seemed to him that his troubles would be over when they emerged from the Atlantic to enter into the great Austral Ocean. The very name Cape of Good Hope made him shiver; in spite of the sad thoughts that assailed him at times, he could not imagine that that name, full of sweet promise, could be a cruel irony. When he thought about it, the black thoughts that pressed upon his brain disappeared immediately, and a violent emotion made his heart beat faster.

His gaze glued to the map, he traced the *Éclair*'s itinerary with a feverish impatience, and submitted his plans to Nicaise and Marcel.

Nothing appeared to him to be simpler than to go from the Cape to the Coral Sea. For him, it was a mater of a week. He did not want to go via the Indian Sea. The best course to reach Botany Bay, where he hoped to obtain information, appeared to him to be directly across the Austral Sea. From Good Hope he would reach the fortieth degree of latitude and would follow it as far as the Bass Strait, situated between Australia and Tasmania. He would pass to the north of Prince Edward Island, Marion Island and the Kerguelen Islands, and also to the north of Amsterdam Island and Saint Paul. The route was, so to speak, already mapped out, and no mistake!

Nicaise and Marcel were in complete agreement, and could only applaud the wisdom of their captain. But the old mariner said to himself that it looked very simple on the map, but it wasn't so easy when one could tangled up in the kelp!

Meanwhile, the *Éclair* was traveling with unprecedented speed—flying, so to speak, over oceanic mountains and valleys.

In spite of the extreme depth of the sea on the Equator, the three voyagers, navigating at more than three thousand meters beneath the surface of the waves, were able, up to a point, to take account of the configuration of the submarine landscapes. Solar light does not penetrate more than five hundred meters, but the vivid gleam of the boat's electric lamp permitted them to distinguish the surrounding terrain with sufficient clarity.

Sometimes, along their course, they were brushing the sharp summits of a mountain chain, sometimes they were gliding, so to speak, over the surface of an immense plateau. Sometimes, they were following broad valleys of enormous depth, whose slopes were carpeted with *Fucus* and *Zostera*. In those immense submarine meadows, innumerable herds of mollusks and zoophytes were grazing. From time to time, the voyagers went down on to the swings in order to get a better view, and the spectacle they contemplated absorbed them to such an extent that they remained there for hours without speaking.

Often, they passed with the rapidity of an express train through the middle of a shoal of fish, in which they made a hole like a cannon-ball in the ranks of an enemy army. Several times they had to fight off hungry dogfish that attacked them, but such combats were mere recreations compared with those in which they had been obliged to engage in the Sargasso Sea.

Trinitus pointed out to his companions how difficult it would be to place a transatlantic cable in the regions they were traversing. Between Newfoundland and Ireland, following great efforts, it had been possible to lay two cables, which functioned marvelously, because in that area the sea covered an immense plateau over which the cables could be drawn and supported, but in the tropics, the bed of the sea is far from being favorable to similar endeavors.

For his part, Marcel observed that the submarine terrain was almost always covered with a layer of white dust, as if it snow had fallen on it. Having collected a small quantity of that dust, Trinitus placed it under the microscope and showed his companions that it was composed of a multitude of imperceptible seashells in a state of perfect conservation.

"Those shells," he told them, "are the debris of animalcules that live in oceanic waters. As they die, their shells fall to the sea-bed, and it is their accumulation, since the world's beginning, that forms the layer of white powder that Marcel has just compared to snow.

"By means of a special sound, developed by the American Brooke,[6] numerous specimens of the infu-

6. John Mercer Brooke (1826-1906) developed his deep-sea sounding device in the early 1850s; it proved invaluable to his patron, the oceanographer Matthew Maury, who sent samples of the material he had dredged up from the Atlantic sea-bed to Jacob Whitman Bailey in 1853, who determined that they were composed of the tiny calcareous shells of Foraminifera. The more general term preferred in France, "infusoria," also embraced the siliceous diatoms to which Trinitus refers.

soria that cover them have been collected from the depths of various oceans. In the Atlantic, as you see, these animalcules have the whiteness of snow. That is because the water of that ocean contain an abundance of calcareous salts, and it's at the expense of those salts that the infusoria build their shells. It's not the same in the Pacific; the dust that covers the bed there is gray rather than white, because silica is more abundant there than calcium, and the shells of the infusoria are silicates.

"When we are thoroughly acquainted with the nature of the animalcules deposited on the sea-bed, we will be able to solve many problems that are presently insoluble. The oceans will have no more mystery for us; the infinitely small will explain the infinitely large!"

# CHAPTER NINE
## THE GOVERNOR OF THE CAPE

In the rapid voyage through the Atlantic, no new obstacle hindered the progress of the submarine boat, and the intelligent pilot of the *Éclair* had the joy of seeing his most ardent wish realized. In three nights and two days, the *Éclair*, admirably steered, reached the thirtieth degree of latitude. He had followed the course of a broad sub-oceanic valley situated between Saint Helena and the coast of Guinea, traveled along its entire length by a branch of the Great Equatorial Current.

The impetuosity of that current, as voluminous as the Gulf Stream, had made a significant contribution to accelerating the velocity of the *Éclair*; Trinitus, as a skillful navigator, had maintained himself in its waters, and after a trouble-free crossing he finally disembarked at the Cape of Good Hope.

The city on the Cape is a strange one. Its inhabitants, who number approximately nineteen thousand, mostly originate from various European countries. One finds Portuguese, Dutchmen, Englishmen and Frenchmen there, mingled with a population of negroes from all parts of Africa.

Sitting at the foot of the high Table Mountain, composed of granite and siliceous sandstone, the town is very well-situated from a commercial point of view, but the new route opened to European vessels through the isthmus of Suez will probably lead to its ruination.

At any rate, Trinitus and his companions moored the *Éclair* under a clump of palm trees about two kilometers from the town, and, as in the Azores, they ate an exquisite meal on the grass.

The scientist, thinking that his sufferings were at an end, was incomparably cheerful. Nicaise and Marcel sang a few patriotic songs and Trinitus joined in with the choruses enthusiastically. The voyagers drank a few toasts to France and to the happy outcome of their voyage, which they hoped to complete in another week.

Trinitus did not want to leave the Cape, however, without going to ask the governor of the town if, by any chance, he had any recent news of the wreck of the *Richmond*. He left Nicaise and Marcel in the shade of the palms, took a decent suit of clothes from the cabin of the *Éclair*, and headed for the town, the first houses of which he could see through the fig-trees and the vines.

He went along a number of streets, very regularly set out, went across a wooden bridge over a small river that descends from the neighboring mountains and finally arrived at a large building, which, he was informed, was the governor's manse.

The scientist went in and a negro domestic asked him

In English whether he desired to speak to the governor. On his affirmative response, Trinitus was led through a large courtyard paced with large granite slabs to the entrance to an interior garden, at the back of which stood an isolated pavilion, covered with wisteria and birthwort.

A man of about fifty, whose face expressed kindness and generosity, was busy writing in a small room situated on the ground floor of the pavilion. He stood up to greet Trinitus, offered him a seat and sat down beside him.

"Monsieur," said the scientist, "can you give me any information about the shipwreck of the English steamer *Richmond*, the debris of which was found a few months ago on the coasts of the Louisiade Archipelago?"

"Yes I can, Monsieur. A ship out of Botany Bay, bound for London, recently brought me details of the terrible disaster."

"Oh, speak, speak!" exclaimed Trinitus, prey to a keen emotion.

"You had relatives aboard the *Richmond*?"

"My wife and daughter."

The governor's expression darkened. "Only seven people have been found at present. They had been able to escape the shipwreck by jumping into a lifeboat, and the tempest pushed them all the way to Wineglass Bay, from which they reached Clarence, then Newcastle, and finally Botany Bay."

Trinitus, his face hidden in his hands, only reacted to the governor's words with a sob.

"However," the latter continued, "other passengers embarked in a second lifeboat. It's certain that they didn't perish with the *Richmond*, but it's not known what became of them. Perhaps they drifted toward the Solomon Islands or the New Hebrides...."

At these words the scientist felt a glimmer of hope revive within him. "Is it known exactly where the ship-wreck took place?" he asked.

"It was in the middle of the Coral Sea," the governor replied, "At approximately fifteen degrees of latitude and 155 of longitude...."

At these words, Trinitus rose to his feet abruptly, as if pushed by a powerful determination. He thanked the governor for the precious information he had just given him, and ran like a madman to rejoin Marcel and Nicaise.

"Good Hope!" he cried to them—and, after telling them the result of his conversation with the governor, he was the first to leap into the *Éclair*.

Five minutes later, the submarine boat was cleaving through the limpid waves of the Austral Ocean, and Trinitus, his eyes glued to the map of the Coral Sea, was interrogating the islands of its numerous archipelagos one by one, as if he might suddenly discover the one where his wife and child were still alive.

# CHAPTER TEN
## THE STORM

Two days after leaving the Cape, the *Éclair* was sailing smoothly in the vicinity of Saint Paul Island when a sonorous and continuous sound suddenly reached the voyagers' ears. It was a sort of dull monotonous rumble, like that of a vast waterfall heard at a distance. The noise became increasingly distinct as the boat moved eastwards.

Initially indifferent to the continuous murmur, Trinitus attributed it to the violence of the wind that must, he said, be blowing over the surface of the sea. When the murmur became a din, however, the scientist could not help feeling a certain anxiety, and he lent his ear to the grim roar, the like of which he had never heard in his life.

Nicaise's cheerful expression darkened, and Marcel felt his heart beating faster. "What is it?" he asked.

"A storm," Trinitus replied.

"Hmm!" said Nicaise. "Probably an out-and-out tempest."

"What does it matter to us, after all?" said Trinitus. "Provided that we can maintain this depth, we have nothing to fear, even from the most terrible storm."

"It's true," Marcel added, "that the *Éclair* is flying like an arrow through calm layers of water, and that we don't feel the slightest agitation."

"God knows, however, that there's agitation above our heads!" said Nicaise. "It must be bad up there!"

"We mustn't forget," Trinitus continued, "that the Cape of Good Hope used to be called the Cape of Storms. The most frightful tempests of all occur in the Austral Ocean."

"Yes, yes," said the old mariner, shaking his head, "That's quite a dance—all the devil's winds must be getting together on the top floor! What a racket! We're lucky to be living in the basement!"

Frightful noises—terrible thunderclaps—punctuated the old mariner's words.

"It's not very reassuring," said Marcel, nervously.

"It's true that a three-master that wouldn't be at ease in that hullabaloo," Nicaise added, insouciantly.

"Instead of easing, the noise is continuing to increase," said Trinitus, and anxiety was also increasing.

"Why, then," Marcel asked, "are tempests so violent in the Austral Ocean?"

"It's because of the frequent conflicts between the atmospheric currents in this region," the scientist replied. "The atmosphere, like the sea, is furrowed in every direction by currents at various levels of temperature, and it's those displacements of aerial fluids that we call the wind. It becomes stronger as the difference in temperature between two opposed currents increases, and in the Austral Ocean, it's the hot air of Africa and the equatorial regions that is in conflict with the icy winds from the South Pole."

The scientist had scarcely finished speaking when the *Éclair*, abruptly deviating from its rectilinear course, veered rapidly and was drawn into a vertiginous movement of rotation.

Taken by surprise, the three men fell over, and Trinitus uttered a cry of fright that chilled his two friends.

"A whirlpool!" he cried and hung on to the wall of the boat as best he could.

An infernal noise—a sort of formidable hissing—resounded in the depths of the immense liquid funnel hollowed out in the waves by the tempest, the side walls of which widened out as they spun. Hazard had determined that the *Éclair* had headed straight into that frightful gulf, and she had been seized and swallowed by the rotating spiral.

In an instant, the most frightful thoughts put the minds of the three companions to the torture.

Borne away by an extraordinary force, deafened by the roar of the hurricane that plunged down in the whirlpool as if it wanted to lift up the entire ocean and rip it from its bed, they spun around and around incessantly, like a pebble in a sling, expecting to see the *Éclair* break up and shatter into a thousand pieces. At times, in the course of that furious rotation, the boat collided with tree-trunks uprooted by the tempest, and Trinitus, his eyes dazzled and his ears full of frightful resonances, heard the vessel's propeller and rudder crack, as a criminal hears the rattle of the tumbrel that will bear him to the scaffold, above the jeers and clamor of the crowd.

Suddenly, however, with a violent clap of thunder that resounded between the sky and the ocean, the whirlpool stopped abruptly, and vanished. Everything that was spinning with it escaped its flanks, and the *Éclair*, badly shaken, disappeared momentarily into a mountain of waves.

Fearfully, Trinitus grabbed the engine lever with a desperate hand—but the boat was no longer obedient to his command. The scientist uttered a cry of rage and despair. The electromotive apparatus had been badly damaged, and the *Éclair*, incapable of continuing her submarine voyage, would be exposed to all the fury of the tempest!

Out of control and completely at the mercy of the ocean, she rose up rapidly to the surface, and was carried away like a cadaver by the exasperated waves.

The terrible hurricane of which it was about to become the plaything was roaring with a frightful racket. Trinitus and his two companions, pale and terrified, waited for death, not pronouncing a single word, and making desperate efforts to hold on to the walls of the cabin, from which frightful shocks threatened to tear them away at any moment.

Everything inside the boat was broken: the apparatus for the manufacture of artificial air; the piles; the instruments, the mechanisms directing the fins and the rudder. Everything had been torn away and smashed. Only the carcass of the boat was undamaged—but the moment would come when, in order to breathe in that enclosed space henceforth deprived of an air-supply, it would be necessary to break one of the portholes.

Trinitus thought vaguely about that supreme resolution, but, in his anxiety, he did not even hope to have to make use of that desperate measure. He expected to be hurled against some rock by the waves at any moment, which would shatter the *Éclair* into a thousand pieces.

The boat was adrift, like an inert mass, driven by the unleashed winds into unknown regions.

Nothing in the world is more formidable than a tempest in the Austral Ocean. The sky and the sea are in conflict, each seeking to wrap itself up, dissolve and drown in the other. The heaped-up clouds tear themselves apart, open up and collapse in a deluge of thunder and lightning, succeeding one another without respite in the midst of the atmospheric torment that seeks to disseminate them in all directions.

The Ocean responds to the thunderclaps and whistling of the gusts of the storm-wind with profound roars. It shakes with indignation, seethes, rises up, tears itself away from its bed and hurls its irritated waves and their invincible crests at the sky. The winds attacking it pierce it and reside its waves to foam; they perforate it with their spirals, as sharp as a drill, hollowing out enormous whirlpools in its flanks and diving furiously into those horrible rotating wounds. In their blind wrath, they tear trees and houses away from islands and continental coasts to crush them in the waves; and those impalpable thieves devastate the land with the ferocity of a hawk stripping the feathers from the warbler that has become its prey.

It was into the midst of such a cataclysm that the *Éclair* was plunged, carrying the unfortunate Trinitus and his friends inside it.

The boat was no longer sailing; she leapt and danced on the waves that lifted her up and drew her along like a piece of cork. She only rose up to the crest of a wave to fall back into a bottomless abyss, from which she rebounded instantly, like a rubber ball hitting the ground. The Ocean made a plaything of her, and the waves tossed her from one to another. She was hurled against them like a shuttlecock against a racket, and after disappearing for a few seconds beneath an avalanche of spray and foam, she reappeared, steaming and whipped by the waters, at the crest of a wave.

Continual flashes of lightning set the atmosphere ablaze, and the thunder never ceased to growl and explode between the sea and the clouds.

The three men, lying face down on the floor of the cabin, were still holding on to projections of the walls in order not to be hurled against one another by the frightful pitching of the vessel.

Marcel, huddling under the table bolted to the floor, had made a cushion of his arm to protect his head from the impacts that threatened it. Similarly, Trinitus and Nicaise had each placed themselves across a porthole, bracing themselves with all their might to avoid the shocks that continually threw them against the walls of the cabin.

From time to time, Marcel uttered a sigh, and Nicaise ground his teeth with rage. Trinitus listened to the formidable voice of the tempest, and, at the risk of being blinded by the incessant lightning, sometimes looked out through the thick windows of the vessel at the furious battle of the sky and the Ocean.

All the electrical and meteorological phenomena to which these terrible cyclones give rise in their hectic course across the sea; all the strange forms that lightning can adopt when it ploughs through the clouds or rips through the atmosphere; all the varieties of flames and gleams that storms engender, from the St. Elmo's Fire that renders the rain luminous to the arborescent flashes whose twenty arms radiate through the air like the tentacles of an immense fiery octopus—in sum, everything grandiose and horrible to which Nature can give birth during the convulsions that agitate her— passed before Trinitus' eyes.

Suddenly, however, a new hubbub even louder and more distinct than that of the tempest made itself heard in the sky. The whistle of the gusts of wind seemed to ease, and was abruptly succeeded by a rattling analogous to that produced by a heavy carriage rolling over cobblestones.

Nicaise, alarmed, pulled his head back into his shoulders like a tortoise retreating into its carapace, and commended his soul to God.

The scientist looked up, and the cry of fright that he

tried to utter caught in his throat.

An immense black cloud was floating like a vulture above the boat. It had the form of a enormous cone, the base of which was lost in the midst of other clouds, and the point of which was pointing down wards, descending slowly toward the vessel in distress.

That frightful cloud, ready to fall upon the *Éclair*, made an immense black patch in the gray and vaporous sky. It was thickening and curling up under the efforts of the tempest; one might have thought that it was swelling up with storms, and that it was charging itself with all the thunder and lightning contained in the neighboring clouds.

All the electricity contained in the atmosphere was condensing in that tenebrous receptacle, in order to burst out all at once. The monstrous cloud was growing more and more horribly as the thunder accumulated in its vast flanks. In its unfathomable depths, a din could be heard resounding like that made by a battery of canons drawn over rocky terrain by thirty horses. From all parts of the horizon, dark cumulus clouds came running to fuse with the enormous cloud and reinforce it. It was a coalition, a mass uprising of al the storms disseminated above the Austral Ocean.

Trinitus was the only person on the boat who saw the formation of that mighty whirlwind, Nicaise and Marcel still being huddled against the walls of the cabin. The scientist, his soul ripped by the keenest anguish, watched the horrible clouds piling up, and wondered anxiously what rebel giant of the heavens could forge such a weapon.

Suddenly, the immense cone that the cloud formed above the *Éclair* writhed in the midst of a squall and extended abruptly under the violent impulsion of the tempest. For its part, the sea abruptly rose up like a mountain, all the way to the underside of the typhoon, and launched itself toward the cloud descending toward it.

The whirlwind breathed in the Ocean.

The cloud, weary of rumbling and blowing the wind, stretched out a gigantic sucker, which had the effect of an enormous leech on the waves. The sea, irritated and furious, was snatched from its bed. The horrible typhoon came lower and lower, rising up at intervals only to descend again a few seconds thereafter, further and for longer. One might have thought it an arm of immeasurable dimensions emerging from the cloud to delve into the entrails of the Ocean.

The latter, increasingly tormented, shivered under the frightful atmospheric disturbance, and followed its monstrous oscillations. When the whirlwind rose up, the livid waves returned to their bed; when it lowered again, they reared up immediately under the suction attracting them.

The two fluid cones had not yet made contact, however. A distance of at least thirty meters separated the summit of the mountain formed by the waves and the monstrous maw of the typhoon, for the latter, in spite of its colossal dimensions, could not fall vertically upon the waves. The wind twisted it and caused it to undulate, without breaking it; it stirred and shook, struggling obstinately against the gusts that bent it incessantly, seeking to break it. One might have thought it an extraordinary serpent hissing with rage, swaying frightfully between the sky and the sea. It was fascinating the Ocean with its terrible gaze, summoning it against its will into its powerful sucker, as a snake attracts a bird.

The formidable column of water suspended from the cloud was perpetually quivering, allowing torrents of vapor to escape from its flanks. The lightning bolts that were flickering at intervals inside it rendered it luminous and made it resemble a glowing river of lava precipitating from the cloud into the sea.

The spectacle, as grandiose as it was frightening, filled Trinitus' soul with both terror and admiration. Still lying on the floor of the cabin, stretching his neck, with his hair bristling and his eyes sparkling, the contemplated all the phases and transformations of the phenomenon, and he waited, in an indescribable anxiety, for the whirlwind and the wave to give one another a frightful kiss.

The boat, paralyzed like the waves by the suction of the typhoon, was no longer able to advance, and the mountain of water formed on the sea held her prisoner on its mobile and crumbling crests.

Meanwhile, the tip of the whirlwind contained to extend, and the entire cloud was about to discharge itself at a single stroke upon the Ocean and the unfortunate vessel. It is true that the *Éclair*, expressly constructed to travel under the water, had nothing to fear from being submerged by the liquid avalanche, but at the supreme moment, Trinitus felt a strange weight upon his chest. He was suddenly out of breath, and was seized almost immediately by a strange vertigo. He heard Nicaise and Marcel sigh. The three unfortunate voyagers, running out of air in the cabin, would perish of asphyxiation if they did not make haste to contrive an opening in the walls of the vessel!

At that frightful thought, Trinitus, no longer thinking about the imminent whirlwind, grabbed a hatchet in order to shatter one of the portholes....

Just as he raised his arm, however, a horrible shock caused him to fall backwards. In a formidable bound, the Ocean had hurled itself into the maw of the typhoon; in the midst of a thunderous collapse and a deluge of winds, the cloud came together with the foaming sea; a column of liquid sixty meters broad united the waves and the clouds!

# CHAPTER ELEVEN
## IN THE ICE

The boat, dragged down beneath the waves to an immense depth by the fall of the whirlwind, rose up rapidly once again through the liquid layers of the Ocean when the frightful typhoon that had been precipitated upon it plunged in its waves. During the few seconds that the abrupt submersion of the *Éclair* lasted, however, the unfortunate voyagers were almost asphyxiated by the unbreathable atmosphere of the cabin, which no longer contained anything but carbon dioxide and nitrogen, gases utterly incompetent, as everyone knows, to maintain pulmonary function.

In order to escape asphyxiation, Trinitus had only found one means; he had resolved to break one of the portholes in order to grant access to the pure and vivifying exterior air. So, as soon as the boat reappeared at the surface of the waves, with a blow of the hatchet that he had grabbed at the moment when the whirlwind fell upon the *Éclair*, the scientist made one of the thick sheets of glass framed in the walls of the vessel explode into fragments.

Immediately, the keen sea air, impregnated with

salty mists and vapors, entered the boat in gusts, and reanimated life in the oppressed torsos of the unfortunate voyagers.

Meanwhile, the tempest, considerably eased by the rupture of the typhoon, gradually diminished in intensity. They sky was uncovered in places, and through the gaps in the cloud, whose last shreds were fleeing rapidly before a stiff north-westerly breeze, Trinitus saw the profound and serene azure of the mysterious region into which the hurricane had thrown his poor boat.

The waves died not die down as rapidly as the thunder and the squalls, however. Although it had exhausted its rage and the efforts of the cyclone, the Ocean was still very agitated. It had difficulty recovering its equilibrium, and was struggling like a man who had just sustained a furious and redoubtable battle. It was still shaking the *Éclair* with extreme violence, causing her to bound over the crests of its waves and driving her into the unknown.

Marcel and Nicaise, exhausted by fatigue, had ended up falling asleep, and even Trinitus, in spite of the abrupt oscillations of the boat, which prevented him from dozing off, felt his eyelids growing heavy.

The scientist had not lost all hope, however. The considerable damage that the *Éclair* had suffered did not worry him overmuch. He knew that the hull of the vessel would resist all the wrath of the Ocean, and he felt sufficient courage to repair the damage inflicted by the tempest, if he had the good fortune to be cast up on land that was not utterly uninhabitable. Science was his good fairy, and Trinitus had extreme confidence in her. He believed that, with her aid, he was stronger than all the conspiratorial elements.

By means of his submarine boat, he had vanquished the Ocean once. The adversary had defeated him in its turn, by breaking the *Éclair*'s powerful electric apparatus, but the scientist counted on getting his revenge one day. With a calm gaze. he contemplated the furious sea that was carrying him away without having disarmed him, seeking to lose him in the most desolate regions in the world, after having tried in vain to drown him in its depths. Impassively, Trinitus allowed it to let out its rage, but with the aid of the map and the compass, he divined its perfidious projects.

The treacherous waves had turned and spun the *Éclair* in vain; they could not disorientate its skillful pilot. His finger placed on the map of the Austral Ocean, he followed the progress of is vessel step by step, and it was him who seemed to be in command of the Ocean, able to push it in one direction or another

He could not help recognizing, however, that his formidable enemy was treating him with the most excessive rigor. The *Éclair* had been carried toward the South Pole, whereas Trinitus would rather have been thrown on to the shore of Australia. It was Botany Bay that he was burning to reach; he felt certain that he would find information there about the wreck of the *Richmond*, and news of his wife and daughter. In spite of these vicissitudes, he had every hope of seeing them again some day.

In the presence of that thought, which never left his mind, the scientist considered with a secret dolor the immense deviation that his boat was making, constantly tossed by the victorious sea. His heart was squeezed by every shock that was dragging her further way from the vicinity of Australia toward the Antarctic polar regions. Fortunately, he maintained his confidence and courage regardless, and it was while thinking of means to repair the *Éclair* on the austral continent that Trinitus, finally vanquished by a great weariness, eventually fell asleep beside Nicaise on the floor of the boat.

The three companions spent the entire night following the day of the tempest and cruel anguish asleep. It was not until the following day, very late in the day, that Nicaise, woken up by the intense cold, was the first to open his eyes.

At the exclamation he uttered, Trinitus and Marcel woke up with a start, and could not retain a cry of surprise and admiration.

The boat was floating on a sea as calm and transparent as crystal, in the depths of a vast crevasse whose walls were formed by gigantic glaciers, which loomed up in the air with thousands of darts, needles and ridges, cut and chiseled in the strangest fashion.

"In what singular country are we going to disembark?" exclaimed Marcel, at the sight of the enormous blocks of ice between which the *Éclair* was imprisoned.

"Are we at the end of the world?" asked Nicaise, shivering.

Trinitus who had not waited to be asked such questions in order to attempt to find out to which point of the glacial Antarctic continent the tempest had had driven them, rapidly concluded the calculation he was already making, and replied: "We're in the region of Victoria Land, discovered by James Ross in 1841, at an approximate latitude of 75° 45′. The continent can't be very far away from our present location. By steering slightly to starboard, we'll discover it...."

"That's impossible," said Nicaise. "We're caught in the ice as if in a vice."

"In that case," said the scientist, "we'll disembark in haste on the enormous block of ice that is blocking the strait in which we're engaged."

"What about the *Éclair*?" asked Marcel. "Are we going to abandon her?"

"Of course not!" said Trinitus. "We're going to hoist her on to the ice and harness ourselves to her in order to take her all the way to the continent."

"Why not simply wait here until we can go on?" asked Nicaise.

"Because we're in extremely great danger between these blocks of ice," Trinitus replied. "These colossal bergs, in the midst of which we're trapped, might suddenly topple over and fall on our heads. The wind might also drive them together, and our poor boat, caught between two massive pile-drivers, would be crushed like a nut between a hammer and an anvil.

Nicaise and Marcel did not ask any further questions. Forced to maintain stout hearts against ill-fortune, the three companions first thought was to put on their thickest garments, in order to resist a mean temperature forty degrees below zero. The woolen blankets were promptly transformed into comfortable burnooses. Trinitus made a kind of cape out of an old fox-fur, with which he covered his shoulders; Nicaise attached a carpet with a pattern of large white and pink roses firmly to his back and breast; and Marcel wrapped himself up in an eiderdown that served to garnish Trinitus' hammock.

These precautions having been taken, the voyagers, happy to have conserved their lives in spite of so many ordeals, in the midst of the dangers they had run, confided themselves once again to Providence, and descended joyfully on to the enormous iceberg against which the *Éclair* was resting.

Immediately, in response to the scientist's proposal, they tried to estimate the extent of the ice-sheet. Having gone up to the culminating point of the iceberg, Trinitus was able to see, with the aid of binoculars, that the island of floating ice on whose summit he was standing was separated from land by a narrow strait encumbered by ice-floes. It was an annoying complication.

After hoisting the boat on to the ice-sheet, it might be necessary to wait for the wind to push it toward the continent, but it would be better to stay on the gigantic iceberg for a day or two than expose themselves to the danger of being crushed by the fall of one of those enormous mountains, which the wind caused to vacillate alarmingly at every moment.

At any rate the ice-sheet seemed very solid, and the scientist did not hesitate to say that it inspired confidence in him. It was a plateau more than four thousand meters in diameter, almost circular, and almost flat over its entire surface. Only at its edges did enormous blocks of ice rise up like the one that Trinitus had climbed—but those steep and menacing blocks appeared to be welded to the sheet, after having floated for a long time in the waters of the glacial ocean.

Hard labor being one of the most powerful means to employ against the cold, the castaways set to work with great activity. In any case, they did not have too much difficulty in dragging the *Éclair* over the iceberg, for the boat was designed in such a way as to roll easily on land, and her small volume, combined with her relative lightness, made the task undertaken by the three companions easy.

Just as they set to work, the wind began to rise, and Trinitus' fears might have ended up being realized but for the promptitude with which he and his friends proceeded with the salvage of the vessel.

In the distance, enormous icebergs were advancing rapidly in the water. Mountains of ice with sharp ridges sheer peaks and flanks pierced by ravines and crevasses of extreme depth, floating islands of all dimensions, ice-floes of a fearsome height, ice-fields loaded with bizarrely-fashioned protrusions—crystal minarets, obelisks, cupolas, bells and porticos—were drifting at the whim of the winds, like the debris of some fantastic planet, heading for the narrow bay in the depths of which the *Éclair* had halted.

Trinitus and his companions cut away ice with hatchets in order to drag the boat on to the sheet more easily. From time to time, when they paused to catch their breath, they looked behind them, at the horizon, to see whether the high mountains of Victoria Land were visible beyond the thick curtain of mist and fog.

# CHAPTER TWELVE
## VICTORIA LAND

After an hour of sustained and obstinate work, a gently-sloping bay had been hollowed out in the enormous berg, which lent itself marvelously to hauling out the boat.

Trintius attached the strongest rope that he could find in the cabin to the base of the prow, and without much effort, Marcel and Nicaise established the poor broken vessel on the ice-sheet.

Meanwhile, the glacial wind blowing from the north was driving the enormous blocks of ice scattered in the sea ever closer to the shore. At times, the floating masses collided with one another with a terrible noise, and some of them, losing equilibrium, capsized in the waves. In the midst of the thick mist that disguised their forms, the formidable bergs resembled moving mountains, collapsing upon one another like Pelion on Ossa.

In the glacial seas that bathe the poles, these frightful combats between icebergs occur frequently. When the wind strengthens slightly, the bergs travel with a velocity of several kilometers an hour. Their steeples sharp and scintillating, their peaks jagged, their edges, carved into battlements, their flanks pierced through or sculpted in a thousand picturesque fashions, they resemble magical edifices, palaces of silver and crystal wandering randomly over an azure ocean.

Woe betide the ship that finds herself caught between these transparent mountains that the wind and the waves precipitate against one another, however! Crushed like a walnut between two enormous stones, she sinks, and is instantaneously swallowed up by the waves.

Having a perfect knowledge of these terrible phenomena, Trinitus had therefore proceeded with the greatest prudence when he had had the boat hauled up on to the ice-sheet. But the scientist was too intelligent to leave it at that. He knew full well that they would not be completely safe until they would be able to set foot on the Antarctic continent, and, without waiting any longer, he wanted to drag the *Éclair* to the opposite side of the iceberg, in order to having nothing more to do but push it on to dry land if the berg were fortunate enough to collide with the shore.

Nicaise and Trinitus therefore harnessed themselves to a cable attached to the anterior part of the boat, and Marcel, stationed at the rear, pushed it vigorously with both hands.

The *Éclair*, resting on the metallic hooks projecting under the keel, yielded easily and slid over the ice as a sled would have done. The ice-sheet, as flat and even as a desert, presented no obstacle to the voyagers' progress.

A pale sun surrounded by the immense colored circles known as haloes, illuminated the little caravan vaguely. Groups of seals lying on the ice, and flocks of gulls and albatrosses bizarrely lined up on the berg's steep crests, watched them go by without manifesting the slightest fear. Cracking sounds could be heard around the sheet, along with sinister splashes and strange noises comparable to the shrill yelping of a litter of puppies, and Trinitus affirmed that the racket was caused by the impacts of colliding ice-floes.

As the voyagers got closer to the edge of the ice-sheet that was facing the continent, the immense field, drifting under the action of the wind, also advanced gradually toward solid ground. The gigantic raft might soon make contact with the coat, and Trinitus counted on taking advantage of that moment to project the *Éclair* on to Antarctic soil. In the presence of this bleak nature and these almost unknown regions, the scientist felt his passion for discovery awakening within him once again, and at times, his scientific projects made him forget his misfortune and grief for a few moments.

However, Nicaise and Marcel broke into his reverie continually with their incessant questions and requests. Where were they going? What would become of them in this desolate country, in which life seemed to be utterly impossible? The boat, transported into a traveling home, contained a good few provisions, but what would they eat when those provisions ran out? Tempests often drove ships into these sad regions of their own accord, but even if they were lucky enough to be picked up by some vessel, would they capable, after a shipwreck, of continuing their journey?

The future, evidently, was very frightening for them—but Trinitus still hoped to be able to repair the *Éclair* and reach Australia in a matter of days, stopping if necessary at a few of the islands scattered in the Austral Ocean.

It was while talking in that fashion that, after an hour's march, the three companions reached the far side of the ice-sheet. A few minutes later, that made contact itself with an enormous table of ice welded to the continent, and, the *Éclair* having been promptly pushed on to that slippery promontory, the voyagers abandoned the iceberg to land on the Antarctic shore.

Gigantic glaciers rose up some distance away like high walls, forming a natural shelter from the glacial wind. The three men took the *Éclair* to the foot of one of those crystalline cliffs, and after having taken all possible precautions to defend themselves against the cold, they went into the boat to rest from the day's exertions.

It is well-known that the nights and days in the polar regions each have a duration of six months, and that when the sun dips beneath the horizon, only to reappear after an absence of a hundred and eight times twenty-four hours, atmospheric phenomena of a dazzling brightness are produced in the sky. These phenomena, known as boreal or austral auroras, according to the pole where they are manifest, are electrical in nature, consisting of luminous fringes, the light of which arrives at intervals to dissipate the horror of eternal night.

Trinitus would have been very interested to see an austral aurora but, according to his calculations, he thought that the daylight would last for another three months, and he hoped to be able to leave Victoria Land long before the end of that interminable day.

After a having slept for a few hours in the cabin of the *Éclair*, carefully padded to prevent the cold from penetrating, the scientist and his friends held a council to determine how they would employ their time in the inhospitable glacial plain of the Antarctic continent.

It was decided that they would occupy themselves first with the repairs to the *Éclair*, and would then set up signals on the culminating points of the shore in order to attract the attention of any navigators who might chance to venture into the glacial Ocean.

The boat was examined thoroughly.

On visiting the electromotive apparatus hidden in the keel, Trinitus discovered, to his terror, that the damage had been much more considerable than he had thought. A long steel rod about as thick as a finger, which formed one of the principal components of the machine, had been broken into three pieces, and no longer permitted the electric currents furnished by the piles and the coils to pass into the mechanisms of the propeller and the pallet-fins. The metal rod in question was, so to speak, the *Éclair*'s spinal cord. It transmitted the electric fluid to the apparatus that moved her, as the nerves conduct nervous fluid to our muscles, and without it, the boat was paralyzed, like a man whose vertebral column is broken.

At that sight, Trinitus uttered a profound sigh, and hid his face in his hands.

Nicaise and Marcel picked up the fragments of the rod and, turning them over in their hands dazedly, gazed at them with the sadness of a child who had just broken his favorite toy.

Meanwhile, Trinitus remained plunged in his reflections.

"It's quite impossible, then," said Marcel, breaking the silence, "to repair this piece of iron?"

"It would be necessary to forge another," the scientist replied.

"And there's no blacksmith around here!" muttered Nicaise.

"If there were only a forge, we could play the smith ourselves," Trinitus replied.

"Well, a forge can be constructed!" exclaimed Marcel, bravely.

"Yes," said Nicaise, sarcastically. "We'll use the wind for bellows, and blocks of ice instead of coal...."

"It's only fuel we lack," the scientist continued. "A block of coal the size of your head could save our lives."

"Strictly speaking, we could replace the coal with wood," said Marcel.

"Of course!" added Nicaise. "We'll get some bundles of firewood from the local charcoal-burner. You're insane! You talk to me about wood and coal, as if we only had to bend down to pick them up—but I'd burn half my body right now, if I were sure of being able to warm up the other half...."

"The fact is," Marcel went on, "that we have to light a fire now or never. The thermometer's forty degrees below zero...."

"We won't find an atom of wood in this region," Trinitus sighed. "At the North Pole one can collect mosses and lichens from the ice—'the last of the vegetables cover the last of the earth there,' as Linnaeus says—but here we won't find any trace of vegetation."

"A charming place!" exclaims Nicaise.

"In that case," Nicaise hazarded, "I propose we ask the sea for the wood that the land refuses us. Tempests are numerous and terrible in the Austral Ocean. Many wrecked ships must have come to break up on these floating glaciers. We're bound to find the debris of wrecks on the coast."

This proposal, daring as it was, won a smile from Trinitus and Nicaise, who had nothing better to suggest. After a meager meal, the voyagers armed themselves with the long hooks that had helped them clear a path through the Sargasso Sea, and, leaving the *Éclair* beside the glacier that sheltered it, they followed the western coast of Victoria Land.

The sea extending to their right was hidden beneath the thick ice that it supported, but its brutal breath numbed Trinitus and drew curses from Nicaise. On the other hand, the icebergs gave the voyagers some protection from the biting wind that blew from the continent. Although they were stopped continually by crevasses yawning before their feet, forced to cling to the ridges of glaciers in order not to slide, and all three of them were shivering and thinking about the dubious prospects of their enterprise, they were not discouraged.

They had been marching for two hours over the blocks of ice without having discovered anything when, having reached the base of an enormous cliff, almost inaccessible from the shore they were on, Marcel uttered a cry of joy and surprise.

"Look! Look!" he cried, drawing his friends' attention to a kind of flag fluttering in the air at the summit of the glacier. And while Trinitus and Nicaise squinted in amazement, Marcel, as agile as a cat, launched himself toward the mountain of ice in order to be the first to reach the torn rag, in which his youthful eyes had recognized the tricolor!

# CHAPTER THIRTEEN
## THE SIGNAL

Finding the French flag fixed to the end of a pole at the summit of a glacier, in an uninhabitable region hundreds of leagues from any settlement, appeared to Nicaise to be one of those events of such extreme improbability that they invite a shrug of the shoulders and a pitying smile.

The thing was, however, real, evident and palpable. It really was the tricolor that was flapping before the eyes of the weary voyagers; it really was the flag of the fatherland that the wind was waving like a joyful appeal at the summit of the ice cliff on the desolate coast of the Antarctic continent.

Greatly excited, Trinitus did not take long to realize that the wind-battered rag was a distress signal, probably planted by castaways on the ice escarpment. Followed by Nicaise, who was having a great deal of trouble recovering from his astonishment, he launched forth after Marcel, and, in spite of the young man's agility, reached the summit of the glacier almost at the same time as him.

The flag was nailed to the tip of a long yard-arm, and

the latter, wedged in the middle of enormous blocks of ice piled on top of one another, had been able to resist the efforts of the wind and to maintain itself almost vertical in spite of the violent squalls blowing from the sea.

Unfortunately, the signal had not been seen by any navigator, for a lantern appeared, visible from some distance away, fixed to the mast beneath the flag, with a bottle beside it containing a scroll of paper.

There, probably was the key to the enigma that was tormenting Nicaise's mind, so the three companions hastened to detach the bottle from the yard-arm and break it, in order to read the document it contained.

With a feverish hand, Trinitus took the paper and unrolled it rapidly. This is what it contained:

> *The French ship* Jenny, *departed from New Caledonia bound for Brest on 22 October, has been driven by a tempest on to the coast of Victoria Land. The crew has just set up this signal on the culminating point of the coast. The* Jenny *is trapped in the ice about three miles to the north. Our provisions have run out; the cold is decimating us. Help us.*

Trinitus finished reading the document with a deep sigh, but Marcel, attentive to nothing but his bravery and devotion, grabbed his friend's hand. "There's no time to lose—let's run!" he said.

The scientist lowered his head, and, with his eyes fixed on the lantern, in which nothing remained but a fragment of carbonized wick, replied in a low voice: "It's too late."

"And besides," Nicaise added, "what could we do for them? Isn't our situation the same as theirs?"

"They're dead," Trinitus continued, distractedly.

"And we won't be long delayed," muttered Nicaise, shivering.

"Come on!" Marcel went on. "We don't know anything! Let's move, damn it! And we won't get cold! The ship must still exist, and we'll find it!"

The last words caused the scientist's pensive face to light up. "Oh! Great God! If the ship exists...."

"Well?" said Marcel.

"Well, we'll be saved. In a matter of hours the *Éclair*, repaired, can take to the sea again!"

"We're leaving!" exclaimed Nicaise. "Oh, I won't miss this place!"

"But the *Éclair* can only carry three people," said Marcel. "What if the crew of the *Jenny* are still alive?"

"Well," said Nicaise, "we'll leave on the sly, without saying anything. Perhaps it's a trifle cowardly, but it's better to leave...."

"Don't talk like that, Nicaise!" Trinitus interjected. "Unfortunately, we'll only find cadavers on the *Jenny*. That empty lantern must have died with the last sailor on the ship. You can take it for granted that that beacon, the only hope of the poor castaways, would have been carefully maintained so long as there was a single living man on the ice...."

Nicaise, blushing at his selfishness, bit his lip—but

as he was better than he seemed, deep down, he shook Trinitus' hand, and said: "You're right. Let's go back to the *Éclair*, and set out in search of the *Jenny*."

The three friends straightened up the yard-arm where the flag was floating, just in case, and went down the slope of the glacier rapidly in order to retrace their route.

After an hour of walking through the ice, a few strange cracking sounds became audible underfoot, and Trinitus thought that he felt two or three volcanic tremors.

Soon, the sky, which was extremely misty to the north, seemed to fill up with smoke; thick clouds accumulated in that direction and dull rumbled resounded in the atmosphere.

"What's that now?" asked Nicaise, surprised.

A formidable explosion replied to him instantly, and a sheaf of flames suddenly appeared in the mists of the distant horizon. The bright light that it projected lit up the sheer peak of a high mountain previously hidden in the mist, vomiting fire.

"A volcano!" exclaimed Nicaise and Marcel, terrified.

"Of course!" said Trinitus, joyfully. "It's Mount Erebus, discovered by James Ross in 1841! Don't be afraid, my friends—it's not malevolent."

It was, indeed, Mount Erebus that had just been suddenly revealed.

The great volcano of the Antarctic pole, rising more than 3,750 meters above sea level, is a gigantic mountain of lava and glaciers. Situated on the seventy-sixth degree of latitude, it offers the frightful contrast of the most ardent fire with the most intense cold. Its base is composed of icebergs, its summit is ablaze. Snow covers its broad flanks and streams of boiling lava streak them. That produces an incessant conflict. At the contact of fire the mountain trembles. It shivers dolorously and roars like a victim of yore tortured with red-hot iron. The incandescent streams of molten basalt sink, whistling, into its rind of ice, like the ardent pincers into the victim's flesh.

Trinitus and his friends contemplated the giant of the austral pole, crowned with a diadem of fire, admiringly. The scientist told Nicaise, who was still a little frightened, how James Ross and his sailors had been able to get quite close to the formidable volcano without running any danger. The bold navigator had realized that the entire mountain was formed of super-imposed layers of basalt and tables of ice. The cold in this region was so intense that the burning lava was not adequate to melt the bed of ice on which it was staunched completely.

While Trinitus was speaking, Erebus rumbled incessantly, and its crater vomited torrents of vapor and intermittent sheaves of flame. The latter reddened the sky on the horizon and the ragged edges of the clouds. The surrounding mountains were gilded by the vast conflagration, like hills by the setting sun, and their snowy summits, their crystal needles and their inaccessible peaks, carved like prisms, reflected the immense blaze with a thousand flashes.

Here and there in that land of fire, other mountains displayed their jagged crests, and they could make out distinctly, alongside Erebus, another extinct crater, probably the one that James Ross had designated by the name of Terror, which he regarded as Erebus' elder brother.

Around the gigantic brazier, like specters surrounding a Sabbat fire, high glaciers still appeared, reminiscent of mighty towers, the multiple ridges of which scintillated in the mist like luminous stripes.

Trinitus paused occasionally to contemplate that grandiose spectacle, and if Nicaise and Marcel had not pressed him to continue on their way, the scientist would have stood there for hours, in ecstasy before the fantastic eruption.

The three voyagers ended up, however, by reaching the cliff at the foot of which they had disembarked, and went back into their mobile home joyfully in order to take a brief rest before setting forth to search for the *Jenny*.

Nevertheless, it was in the evening of the same day that they began that adventurous expedition. The *Éclair*, dragged by Trinitus and Nicaise, slid once again over the ice, following the northern coast of the continent.

Given that the *Jenny* was trapped in the middle of an ice-sheet three miles from the cliff where the signal had been set up, Trinitus thought that it would be better to leave the *Éclair* at the foot of the glacier than to be inconvenienced by it while searching for the wrecked ship.

Marcel and Nicaise accepted this proposition, and when the caravan had reached the foot of the cliff Trinitus' amphibious boat was lodged in a fissure in the glacier, sheltered from the sea-wind that was driving the icebergs and floes toward the continent.

Then the three men, exhausted by fatigue, went into the cabin and slept profoundly for a few hours.

Meanwhile, Mount Erebus, after having vomited lava and swirls of smoke for a long time, gradually calmed down, and its dull growling ceased to be audible.

The eruption was reaching its end when Trinitus woke up, but, even though the volcano was more than thirty kilometers away, the scientist noticed that a thin layer of ash was covering the immense icy plain that extended between the coast and the first mountains of the continent. During his sleep, that ash, vomited by the crater, had settled gently on the ground.

When Nicaise, fully armed, came out of the cabin in his turn to go in search of the Jenny, the sight of that vast sheet of dust, laid like a carpet of the glacial desert, struck him with surprise and extracted an emotional tear from him.

Trinitus and Marcel, observing his emotion but being unable to deduce its cause, asked him what as wrong.

"I've just realized," the old mariner replied, "why the good God put volcanoes in this place."

"Damn!" said Trinutus. "I'd like to know that

myself."

"Well, it's obvious," the fellow added, with a smile. "It's simply to throw the ash on to the ice, in order that brave men who go in search of ships don't run the risk of slipping and breaking their backs!"

"Right!" said Trinitus. "It's not the most scientific of explanations, but it's no worse for that!"

# CHAPTER FOURTEEN
## THE CADAVER ON THE SHIP

In accordance with the indications furnished by the document written by the castaways of the *Jenny*, Trinitus searched for the ship at the northern end of the cliff, through the enormous icebergs that the wind had had driven toward the coast. The search was extremely difficult. To reach the sea, which was continually masked by blocks of ice of prodigious height, it was necessary to climb over all the accessible peaks, and as they were generally the lower ones, one could only discover a very limited horizon from their summits.

It was continually necessary to follow veritable alleyways hollowed out in the ice, the sheer walls of which, taller than six-story houses, limited the view in all directions. A host of insurmountable objects also stopped the explorers repeatedly. Sometimes it was a broad and deep crevasse that opened before them, sometimes a snowdrift into which they sank waist-deep and forced them to retreat.

From time to time, in order to attract the castaways' attention, if, by chance any still remained on the *Jenny*, the three men uttered formidable hurrahs, followed by a simultaneous discharge of their firearms. The echoes of the glaciers, in prolonged and peculiarly sonorous resonances, multiplied the shots and magnified the sound of the detonations, but no other sound replied to those frequent appeals.

Trinitus was beginning to believe that not only had the entire crew of the *Jenny* died of cold and deprivation, but that the ship itself, probably crushed between two ice-sheets, had disappeared under the waves.

After thirty-six hours of stubborn research, however, Marcel, having scaled a cliff that Nicaise and Trinitus had identified as an excellent observatory, a black dot framed by an ice-field suddenly struck his gaze. The distance that separated him from that dot was so considerable, though, that he needed to have recourse to Trinitus' binoculars to determine exactly what he was looking at.

Scarcely had he raised the optical instrument to his eyes than a cry of victory escaped his lips. "I can see the ship! I can see the *Jenny*!"

The cheers and enthusiastic shouts of Trinitus and Nicaise welcomed that good news; the two mariners assured themselves of the *Jenny*'s position, wedged in the ice as if in a vice, and the little troop, alert and joyful, headed toward the wrecked ship at top speed.

Soon, the three companions came into the icy plain that extended as far as the eye could see around the *Jenny*, and from then on they were able to study the unfortunate vessel at their ease.

She was a brig of the most wretched appearance.

Her masts had been sawn off at deck level and her hull had been badly dented by the violent impacts of the icebergs and floes in the midst of which she had been sailing. Here and there, her split sides gaped open, seemingly covered with hideous wounds. On the ice, at the foot of the ship, fragments of planks, scraps of sails, fishing equipment and a few tools had been abandoned, half-hidden in the snow. Ends of rope hung down everywhere; a narrow ladder had been set up beneath an open hatchway.

Before climbing up, Trinitus and Nicaise hailed the crew several times. With Marcel they made a circuit of the ship, but, no one having responded to their reiterated appeals, they decided to climb up on to the deck.

Suddenly, Trinitus, having looked curiously through a porthole, uttered a cry of amazement and fright. His two friends wanted to see too, and they perceived a man sitting in a cabin at a small table laden with ledgers and papers.

In spite of the secret terror that took possession of them at that sight, they did not hesitate to continue the exploration that they had commenced, and as soon as they had reached the deck they hastened to clear away the snow accumulated at the head of the stairway. They descended into the cabins with an urgency mingled with keen anxiety, and immediately headed for the room occupied by the mysterious individual they had see through the porthole.

Trinitus opened the door. The man was sitting in the same place, still immobile. The scientist approached him and took his hand; it was stiff and icy. A greenish moisture covered his pale lips and veiled his eyes; his right hand, leaning on the table, was holding a pen, and a voluminous journal was open before him.

While Trinitus recognized, trembling, that the unfortunate man had been killed by the cold, Marcel cast his eyes over the last lines that the hand had written, and read in a high voice:

> *Seventeenth January. It's now thirty-three days that our ship has been trapped in the ice. Our fire went out yesterday evening and the captain tried in vain to relight it. His wife died this morning of cold and hunger, along with five crewmen. No more hope!*

On hearing those words, Trinitus cast his eyes over the journal, but suddenly, recoiling fearfully, he fell into Nicaise's arms, uttering a terrible cry. He had just perceived a casket on the table that he had seen before, in the hands of his daughter—and, indeed, on which the name *Alice* was inscribed in golden letters.

His amazement was, it is true, of short duration.

The scientist launched himself toward the box like a miser hurling himself on a treasure. He took it in his hands and sprinkled it with his tears, kissing it rapturously.

Nicaise and Marcel, as astonished as he was, shared his emotion and felt a new courage reborn within them.

On opening the casket, however, Trinitus suddenly went pale. A shiver made his entire body tremble.

Seized by fear, he wondered whether the letter that his fingers felt inside the box might suddenly strike him a mortal blow by revealing the most fatal news to him.

It was a terrible moment of anguish for the poor scientist, when, with a tremulous hand, he opened the mysterious note over which he dared not cast his eyes. Suddenly, however, a glint of joy made his face radiant, and his heart beat faster. In the blink of an eye he passed from the most atrocious doubt to the most ardent hope. He was completely transfigured.

The note contained in the casket was written in Alice's handwriting. A few lines were traced in pencil.

> *The English steamer* Richmond *has been broken by a tempest in the Coral Sea. Ten passengers saved in a lifeboat have jut disembarked on the coast of an island that is unknown to them, but must belong to the archipelago of the New Hebrides. May God protect them, while waiting for their brethren to come to their rescue.*

"Finally!" cried Trinitus. "The tempest has spared my dear child! She's alive! And her mother is doubtless alive too! Oh, Nicaise...Marcel...what joy for us! Be brave, and we'll find them. By virtue of strength and energy, we'll triumph over all obstacles! We'll be stronger than all the elements conspiring against us!"

Nicaise and Marcel shook their friend's hand effusively.

"Dear child," Trinitus went on, emotionally. "How

far she must have been from suspecting, when she wrote this note, that it would be read by her father! Do you understand exactly how it has fallen into our hands? It's the currents that flow from the Coral Sea to here that have carried it this far. The *Jenny* was already trapped in the ice when her passengers picked up the casket! Perhaps there's even mention of it in the log—isn't there, Marcel?"

The young man, who had just picked up the journal from the table, turned two or three pages and suddenly exclaimed: "Eighth January. This morning a sailor brought back a box thrown into the sea by castaways. May they be more fortunate than us, and escape the frightful death that awaits us."

"Poor fellows," said Trinitus, gazing once again at the pale face, hardened by cold, of the unfortunate man that death had nailed to the chair beside the table. "What frightful tortures they must have endured!"

Thinking, however, that he would probably find all the tools necessary to repair the *Éclair* in the carpenter's locker, the scientist soon hastened to get out of that funereal cabin, to the great relief of Nicaise and Marcel.

Following the corridors of the ship, the three men discovered four more cadavers stiffened by the cold but retaining all the appearances of life.

The *Jenny* seemed to be a vast sepulcher, and the ice-field in which she was imprisoned rendered it a hundred times more sinister than the darkest tomb.

Nicaise marched in terror over the sonorous planks,

Marcel dared not proffer a word, and Trinitus, having occasionally had the audacity to open a door, hardly ever closed them again without a secret surge of fear.

The cadavers of the *Jenny* were, in fact, veritably fearful. The majority of the passengers, having expired in atrocious suffering, had retained on their faces the horrible expression of pain, and one might have thought that death, by virtue of a refinement of cruelty, had taken pleasure in conserving the features of his victims, in order to see engraved there the marks of the most frightful agony.

Finally, after some groping, Trinitus and his two companions arrived at the master carpenter's cabin. There was no cadaver there, and all the tools were in their usual places. A little forge devoid of fuel appeared in a neighboring cabin, the partition wall of which had been broken, probably in order to be burned. At that sight, the scientist uttered a cry of joy, and while Nicaise broke up an old table in order to make a fire, he set about searching the drawers and chests for a metal rod that could replace the *Éclair*'s broken axle.

After a few minutes he was fortunate enough to discover a steel bar that seemed to possess all the desirable qualities, and Marcel presented him with a box of files that he welcomed with the greatest pleasure.

Soon, thanks to Nicaise's perseverance, flame sprang up in the forge, the steel bar was reddened in the fire, and Trinitus fashioned it as he wished on the anvil, striking it with a hundred mighty hammer-blows, as if he wanted to wake the dead men that the *Jenny* retained in her flanks.

# CHAPTER FIFTEEN
## NEW ZEALAND

The scientist required no less than six hours of patient and continuous work to forge the metal axle that would render the power of movement to the paralyzed *Éclair*. At the end of that time, however, Trinitus, delighted at having succeeded, was able to show his work proudly to his companions.

The others, seeing in that simple metal rod the key to the prison of ice into which the tempest had cast them, wanted nothing more than to quit the *Jenny* in order to depart with the *Éclair* in search of the castaways of the *Richmond*.

Marcel carried Alice's casket preciously. Trinitus took a few tools and the axle he had fabricated with his own hands. Nicaise loaded himself with a few earthenware jars found in the medicine cabinet and a large glass plate intended to replace the window of the *Éclair* that Trinitus has broken after the descent of the whirlwind.

Thus equipped, the three men abandoned the unfortunate ship of which cold and deprivation had made a floating cemetery, and over which the icy winds of the pole were gradually depositing a thick shroud of snow.

The repairs to the *Éclair* did not take long. The axle forged by Trinitus fitted marvelously into the place of the one that had been broken, and a few thrusts with a file made the adaptation perfect. The piles were refilled with copper sulfate and the powerful coils that multiplied the force of the electric current were reinstalled in the keel of the submarine boat. The apparatus for the manufacture of the artificial atmosphere was reestablished by Trinitus, and Marcel took charge of its supervision again.

The ropes supporting the swings suspended beneath the boat, the diving-suits and the rubber tubes designed to draw air from the cabin, the valves of the cylindrical corridor by means of which they descended on to the swings without water penetrating the ship, and, in sum, all the delicate components of the *Éclair* were successively subjected to Trinitus' minute inspection.

After a frugal meal, the three men harnessed themselves to their moving house once again and dragged it to the edge of the sea in order to set it afloat. Intoxicated by joy, Nicaise and Marcel went aboard first, and Trinitus, leaving the Antarctic land after them, sent a last salute to the flamboyant summit of Erebus, which was standing out majestically on the misty horizon.

In order not to run the risk of colliding with an icefloe during his passage, and to avoid the *Éclair* being crushed between the icebergs, the scientist immersed the boat immediately, and it was swallowed up by the waves of the glacial sea.

The temperature of the circumpolar waters being much higher than that of the austral regions themselves, Trinitus and his two friends enjoyed a sense of wellbeing aboard that was all the more agreeable because they had not anticipated it. The relief that they felt in fleeing that desolate country, where they would soon have perished of hunger and cold, was inexpressible. Marcel and Trinitus built a mountain of charming projects, and Nicaise hummed the refrains of old songs while gesticulating—which, in him, characterized the highest degree of contentment.

In order to reach the archipelago of the New Hebrides—where, according to the letter found in Alice's casket, the castaways of the Richmond must have landed—more rapidly, the scientist had mapped out a route through the Antipodes Islands, the Cook Strait between the two islands of New Zealand, the small Norfolk Island and the eastern tip of New Caledonia.

The Cook Strait was the central point of that long journey, but making a landfall there was not without danger, because of the ferocity of the natives of New Zealand, who would gladly devour all the voyagers if they were able to capture them. After having passed the inhospitable rocks of the Antipodes Islands, however, Trinitus was soon obliged to take the *Éclair* up to the surface, because of the perpetual threat of collision with the sea-bed and the madreporic reefs neighboring the southern entrance of the Cook Strait.

Scarcely had that maneuver been executed than the

three navigators were able to see the high mountains of Ika Na-Mawi, the northern island of New Zealand, including the snowy peak of Mount Egmont, more than three thousand feet above sea level.

As they approached, more of the land was gradually revealed, displaying magnificent locations and delightful landscapes to their eyes. Streams descending from the mountains ran through valleys and plains planted with clumps of breadfruit trees and gigantic banana-trees. Forests of cedars and coconut palms covered the hillsides. The coast was shaded by extraordinary vegetation, and among the reeds, bamboo and papyrus that flourished in the dense grasslands, flocks of red flamingos appeared, fishing on the edges of the streams.

At the sight of that Eden, so different from the icy regions of the Antarctic continent, the three friends were gripped by admiration. Nicaise would have liked to land briefly in order to take a siesta beneath a clump of palm tress, but Trinitus and Marcel, no longer thinking about anything but the New Hebrides, persuaded their comrade that he would inevitably be devoured by cannibals, so effectively that the old mariner, terrified, no longer wanted anything except to get through the Cook Strait as rapidly as possible.

# CHAPTER SIXTEEN
## A DUEL OF GIANTS

Having come through the narrow passage separating the two halves of New Zealand without incident, the *Éclair* was traveling at a fearsome speed beneath the warm tropical waves between Norfolk Island and the New Caledonian Isle of Pines when Marcel thought he could hear a muffled bellowing some distance away that was not unfamiliar to him.

Trinitus and Nicaise, entirely engrossed the joy induced by the hope of an imminent disembarkation, immediately lent their ears to it, and the scientist suddenly leapt toward the electric motor to interrupt the progress of the vessel. Nevertheless, the *Éclair*, which was moving parallel to the crest of a series of submarine hills, had time to arrive over a kind of valley, in the depths of which the most formidable conflict that it is possible to envision was taking place.

A whale at least twenty meters long was at grips with another animal, equally enormous and monstrous but more terribly armed.

The body of that ferocious combatant, covered with a tough and oily skin, was both as strong as an oak and as supple as an osier. Its caudal extremity was terminated by a large muscular fluke lashing and cutting through the water like the rudder of a ship. Its head, small and round, scarcely distinct from the neck, presented two piercing black eyes full of anger, and directed beneath those eyes a narrow red-tinted crack was alternately opening and closing, growling furiously. It was the mouth, ridiculously small and almost deformed by comparison with the colossal dimensions of the body.

Very large in its mid-section, the monster was considerably tapered at its two extremities, bearing a rough resemblance to a spindly. The posterior end, armed with the fluke, was writhing and describing undulations like a snake; the anterior end, commencing at the truncated tip of the muzzle, was elongated, as rigid and inflexible as a steel bar, for a length of three meters. It was an ivory tusk as thick as an arm, as hard and solid as a granite needle, and as sharp and piercing as a sword-blade. Its base was welded to the bronzed forehead of the animal, which used that weapon as swordsman uses his blade.

It was fighting and thrusting hectically, sometimes blindly and randomly, hardly brushing the whale—which took evasive action—with every thrust, and almost always colliding with branches of coral, which shattered under its blows.

Trinitus had no difficulty recognizing, by virtue of that form and the characteristic tusk, one of the most redoubtable inhabitants of the seas, the narwhal—

Linnaeus' *Monodon monoceros*—the famous marine unicorn of the romancers of the Middle Ages. He knew how horrible the battles were that were fought against whales by that mysterious and almost mythological mammal; he knew about its strength and audacity, and was not unaware that a large number of vessels attacked in the open sea by herds of narwhals had been holed by the tusks of those terrible animals.[7]

So, dreading that the unicorn that was fighting before his eyes might turn against the *Éclair* in its blind rage, the scientist strove to maintain the boat at a respectful distance from the two antagonists.

At the sight of that frightful struggle, however, Nicaise felt the ardor of his youth reanimated within him. Remembering that he had once made war against whales in the seas of the Arctic circle, and in spite of Marcel's pleas and Trinitus' advice, he wanted to go down on to a swing in order to attempt to kill the narwhal with a thrust of the electric harpoon.

While he put on his diving-suit, armed himself from head to toe and slid into the cylinder with the valves in order to install himself on one of the seats suspended from the *Éclair*, the whale attacked by the unicorn defended itself with increasing boldness and obstinacy.

The enormous cetacean, having no offensive weapon in its armory, limited itself to warding off the thrusts

7. Narwhals are not native to the Coral Sea, and are relatively modest in size, but a rich mythology had grown up around them because of the roaring trade in narwhal tusks—usually sold as "unicorn horns" by whalers, who were doubtless ingenious in embroidering accounts of their provenance—without which no eighteenth-century "cabinet of curiosities" could be considered complete.

that its ferocious adversary was incessantly directing against it. The sea quivered and vibrated under the vigorous thrusts of the caudal fluke; clicking sounds and prolonged grating sounds, like those produced by the abrupt tearing of silken fabric, accompanied all the shocks and contractions of its body. Its eyes were shining with terror, and its blow-holes, frightfully dilated, were panting like a storm wind and making the sea seethe.

The narwhal was rushing with an extraordinary impetuosity against the animate mass, which was growling like thunder, slipping away at every blow with the agility of a bird. By its rapid movements and its instantaneous swerves, the frightful colossus rendered itself impalpable and almost invisible. The unicorn's tusk was still striking empty water or hitting the wrong target.

The battle only became fiercer, however, and the spectators were expecting to see the narwhal open the belly of the whale at any moment when Nicaise suddenly appeared on the swing, holding the electric harpoon in a threatening manner.

Marcel and Trinitus, breathless and gripped by fear, instinctively squeezed one another's hand. They experienced an indescribable anguish.

Suddenly, a lightning-bolt sprang from the bosom of the waters; the sound of a thunderclap, followed by a noise similar to that produced by the fall of a stream of lava into the sea, resounded in their ears. The boat recoiled abruptly and the most frightful silence succeeded the paroxysm of the battle and the terror.

The swing was empty. Nicaise and the two combatants had disappeared!

# CHAPTER SEVENTEEN
## THE CORAL SEA

It is easy to imagine the consternation and dolor experienced by Trinitus and Marcel, when they could no longer see the brave Nicaise, the excellent friend who had not hesitated to share their struggles and sufferings, the devoted companion whose sage advice had been so useful to them on many occasions.

Their hearts oppressed by the most poignant emotion, their eyes bathed in tears, and their breasts elevated by sobs, the two men, breathless, trembling, and bewildered, carried out the most scrupulous search, but in vain.

Vainly, Trinitus took the *Éclair* in all directions; vainly, he explored the rocky fissures of the sea-bed; vainly, he took the boat up to the surface to make sure that Nicaise had not floated upwards, unseated by the terrible animals that he had tried to combat. All his maneuvers were futile; the old mariner did not reappear, and his companions did not even find his corpse.

What had become of poor Nicaise? Only one hypothesis was admissible in response to that terrible question. It was probable that the narwhal, attacked by the mariner and struck by the electric harpoon, had had time to turn on its aggressor and transpierce him with its redoubtable tusk. Nicaise, run through, must have been snatched from the swing and dragged far away beneath the waves by the victorious monster.

After a day of fruitless explorations, Trinitus and Marcel stopped, discouraged by that frightful thought, and, realizing that there was no point in searching for their companion any longer, they sadly redirected the *Éclair* toward the New Hebrides, and did not take long to arrive in the limpid waters of the Coral Sea.

How charmed their souls would then have been, had they not been racked by the most intense grief! Beneath the waves they were traversing, a fantastic and seemingly almost supernatural world suddenly opened up before their eyes.

They had entered into the magical world where, for thousands of years, innumerable legions of zoophytes had been laboring to build a continent in the middle of the sea. Around the *Éclair*, in every direction, as enormous and majestic as the oaks of a dense forest, stony trees rose up, as hard and white as ivory.

The dimensions of these colossal pillars were incalculable. Their bases, as broad as that of a pyramid, each supported the entire surface of a submarine plateau; their cavernous flanks, hollowed out like the bell-tower of a Medieval church, enclosed constellations of curious animals, framed in iridescent nacre or the red of corals like diamonds in the gold of a brooch. An envelope as transparent and tremulous as a jelly coated the vast trunks and impenetrable branches of the petrified trees like a crystalline bark, and buds of every color blossomed like foliage at the extremities of their branches. Far from having the simple organization of a vegetal tissue, however, these multicolored buds were animate creatures, intermediate between animals and plants, and, whereas trees produce the leaves with which they are covered, these bizarre beings had, on the contrary, slowly built the enormous stone vegetables from which they were suspended.

Trinitus was not unaware that these zoophytes, so various in form and type, although generally described by the name of polyps, had between working constantly for many centuries on the cyclopean work that his eyes beheld, but the work was so grandiose, surpassing to such an extent, even in its smallest details anything that the human imagination could conceive, that the scientist, stupefied in the presence of such a spectacle, sensed his faith become unsteady in spite of his reasoning.

He was witnessing the construction on the seabed, by a formless animalcule, of an immense continent.

That forest of calcareous concretions, marble pillars, coral columns and pedestals, madrepores and polyparies, was the base of a future country, a world to come. The diaphanous and gelatinous polyp, both the architect and mason of these immense submarine projects, was preparing a new land beneath the veil of the waters for beings more perfect than itself.

The salts of the sea, constantly separated by the

zoophyte from the waves that held them in solution, are the materials employed for the foundation of these oceanic lands, which are rising up day by day, and whose principal summits have already pierced the blue sheet of the Pacific Ocean. A multitude of islands, characterized by their annular form, constantly surge forth beneath the blazing tropical sun and form barrier reefs in the first days of their infancy, against which ships often break up.

Born, like Amphitrite, from the bosom of the waves, these white and virginal islands contrast with the lava rocks and volcanic peaks engendered in other oceans by sub-oceanic craters. Their pure, soft and friable soil turns brown, like a child's skin, in broad sunlight, but as it is extremely fertile, Nature, which sows life everywhere, does not leave it idle for long.

The winds transporting seeds of every sort through the atmosphere, soon passing over the island, astonished to find it above the water, lavish their warm caresses upon it. At those unfamiliar kisses, on contact with that embalmed and fecundating breath, the virginal earth suddenly shudders and quivers. It feels roots slowly elongating in its bosom, and life circulating like a generous blood in its entrails. It dilates and rejoices in the heat of the sun; it loves the warm breath of the breeze, covering itself with somber forests full of nests and flowers; it becomes the mother of a paradise.

The *Éclair* advanced slowly through the tortuous pathways of the bushes of coral, and as it plunged further on beneath those ivory vaults, covered in living enamel, the submarine landscape changed its appearance and become increasingly grandiose.

The pillars and columns took on increasingly colossal dimensions; the arches, porches, balustrades and buttresses multiplied infinitely, interlacing in a thousand picturesque fashions; the branches of gigantic polyparies joined up to form vast porticos, and by degrees, the immense forest of madrepores changed into an enchanted palace.

In that extraordinary architecture, hazard combined the most audacious lines and the most extravagant forms, and yet, the result was an admirably harmonious ensemble. Nothing their offended the sight, nothing made itself remarkable by its pettiness. The slightest details of that work, begun at the origin of the world and perhaps destined only to end with it, charmed Trinitus' observant mind, and struck it with a profound astonishment.

In every direction the scientist perceived, heaped and grouped with a perfection that only Nature can attain, ornaments and embroideries of stone sculpted in all proportions and according to every style. There was not one slightly projecting ledge that was not graciously carved, not one fissure that was not hollowed out as if by the mot skillful of artists.

And yet, the authors of these incomparable marvels had followed no guide, no rule and no law. The gelatinous mouth of the polyp, the solvent kiss of the water and the friction of the waves had accomplished that prodigious task on their own.

But these sub-oceanic edifices are not only inhabited by the laborious workers that continue their interminable construction every day. All that the Indian Ocean contains of zoophytes, annelids, mollusks and curious fish come together in the meanders and madreporic galleries of the Coral Sea. All the radial animals, the heads and organic bodies of which are welded to feet of stone, live there. Sea anemones deploy their brilliantly colored tentacles there, blossoming in the excavations of polyparies like magnificent dahlias in vast baskets. Lithophytes and branching *Caryophyllia* raise their thousand arms there, and the lacy networks of *Retipora* are covered by clumps of sponges, *Bryozoa* and *Astraea*. Republics of *Alcyonacea* prosper there, and *Gorgonia* of all shades affix their large fans there.

At times, these immobile tribes of animate flowers shiver and seem to emerge from their mysterious torpor. The unknown spell that weighs upon them ceases, as if by magic, and all the creatures plunged in the liquid azure of the Ocean wake up, shivering. Life suddenly appears to spring forth from their translucent, almost immaterial bodies; luminous beams and phosphorescent aureoles radiate in all directions, and while darkness expends over the surface of the waves, the depths of the sea, as well as the celestial spaces, light up with a thousand gleams. Then the blue-tinted *Aequorea*, the *Rhizostoma* and the medusas, expanding their flesh umbrellas, stroll nonchalantly through the waves; the sea-urchins and starfish spangle the bed, and the madreporic constructions; the entire sub-oceanic world agitates, as if in response to the world of stars—and the splendors of the sea, as well as those of the sky, are only extinguished by the rays of the rising sun.

Trinitus and Marcel traveled for nearly two days in the midst of all these marvels. But the magnificence of the spectacles that struck their eyes did not ease their dolor. The admirable Coral Sea was merely terrible and cruel to them. First it had swallowed the *Richmond*, now it had drowned Nicaise and buried him forever in its tenebrous caverns.

However, the *Éclair* had doubled the eastern point of New Caledonia and, according to Trinitus' calculations, it was probably not far from Anatom and Tanna, the first of the New Hebrides. The scientist immediately surfaced, and the boat, sparkling in the sunlight, sailed north-eastwards for some time.

In this region, the waves had a reddish tint, due to numerous animalcules that sometimes rise to the surface from the depths of the sea, and of which several navigators have observed numerous species, but the remarkable phenomenon did not interest Trinitus much. The elevated coasts of an island were visible on the horizon and the scientist's heart was beating violently. Perhaps it was there that his dear Alice was still alive, in company with her mother; perhaps, on that isolated corner of land, he would finally be able to take his wife and child in his arms.

Suddenly, a dark thought went through Trinitus' mind. He knew about the ferocity of the indigenes of

New Caledonia, and was not unaware that those of the New Hebrides were just as cruel as their neighbors.[8] In consequence, before disembarking on the island that he was approaching, the scientist wanted to make his preparations for war. While Marcel equipped himself with two shotguns and a revolver, Trinitus armed himself with the rifles he had bought before leaving France, and a magnificent hunting knife, which he stuck in his belt in the guise of a sword.

---

8. The reputation for ferocity and cannibalism foisted upon the natives of New Hebrides (nowadays the Republic of Vanuatu), fostered by travelers' tales and missionary propaganda, helped to provide an excuse for their ruthless exploitation. Following the discovery of sandalwood in the New Hebrides in 1825 there was a sudden influx of immigrants, against whom the natives rebelled. At the time the story is set in the 1860s, the New Hebrides and other Polynesian archipelagoes were active centers of the practice of "blackbirding"—the recruitment of indentured laborers by force or fraud— which partially replaced the supposedly-abolished slave trade.

# CHAPTER EIGHTEEN
## ON CAMPAIGN

It was with a profound emotion that Trinitus and Marcel landed on the unknown island, so beautiful and cheerful beneath the crowns of the trees shading it that it seemed to have adorned itself expressly to welcome them.

A narrow bay veiled by thick clumps of bamboo and mangroves served the *Éclair* as a harbor, and as soon as they set foot on the ground, the two men attached the submarine boat solidly to the trunks of a few small trees. Then, placing themselves under the protection of Providence, they resolved to devote at least two days to the exploration of the island. In order to obtain a general idea of the lie of the land, they decided to climb to the summit of a high hill whose flanks, clad in a luxuriant vegetation, descended gently to the sea shore.

Their ears attentive to the slightest sound, eyes on the alert, and weapons in hand for fear of a surprise attack, they went into a wood of coconut palms and breadfruit trees, their souls prey to the sharpest emotions, and advanced prudently into the interior of the island.

The hillside, hollowed out in places by torrential

tropical rain, was pitted by broad rents bristling with rocks spurs, the irregularly-formed edges of which formed a multitude of retreats and shelters. These broken-walled ravines plunged like sunken roads into the shade of the gigantic plants that covered them, and legions of tall herbaceous plants grew in the yellow sands accumulated at the bottom of the vast furrows carved through the clay.

A continuous buzzing was audible in the woods. It was the sound of the wings of large butterflies and beetles, punctuated periodically by the whistle of a mockingbird or the rapid rustle of leaves caused by a frightened lizard.

The sky was intensely blue, and the sun inundated the ground with light, causing the flowers of the large plants that poured their benevolent shade on the ground to blossom almost visibly.

Trinitus and Marcel, dazed by the beauty of the landscape, marched side by side, enduring the heat without complaint, resigned to making occasional long detours when impenetrable thickets of thorny plants blocked their way. Trinitus, very knowledgeable in botany, was delighted to see the superb vegetation of the tropics in all its splendor, which he had only studied previously in albums and books. His pleasure was extreme when he recognized them by courtesy of his memory alone. Sometimes he stopped in front of a magnificent sago-palm; sometimes he contemplated the arches of verdure formed by the bold interlacements of birthwort and wisteria; sometimes he waxed ecstatic before a wax-tree, a cachou areca, a thick-stemmed euphorbia or a nutmeg-tree. He formulated admirable theories regarding a sensitive plant that he brushed against, and by means of irrefutable arguments, demonstrated to the enthusiastic Marcel that *Piper methysticum*, from which the people of Oceania extract an intoxicating sap, bore no similarity at all to the *Piper betle*, which furnishes the numbing narcotic known as betel.[9]

After marching for a few hours, the two companions arrived at the top of the hill, and the panorama revealed to them at that culminating point redoubled their admiration.

The entire island was buried under foliage; only a few sheer peaks emerged at intervals, their sharp spires piercing the immense sheet of verdure extended at their base.

Trinitus and Marcel were extracted from the ecstatic contemplation into which they had been plunged by guttural and sinister cries that caused them to shiver. The screams seemed to emerge from a human throat, and were coming from the extremity of a valley separated from the sea by the hill that the two voyagers had just climbed.

More surprised than frightened, Trinitus and Marcel looked at one another hesitantly for a moment, but all of a sudden the same thought occurred to them both,

---

9. Rengade gives the former species as "*Macropiper methusticum*," perhaps having confused it with *Macropiper excelsum*—which is not found in Vanuatu—also known as kawakawa. *Piper methysticum* is the much better-known kava. *Piper betle* is a closely-related vine-like plant, the lack of similarity pertaining to their medicnal extracts, kava being a sedative and betel a stimulant.

and their eyes shone with a wild gleam.

"Perhaps Alice is down there!" Marcel murmured, shivering.

"Let's run!" exclaimed Trinitus—and, shaking his companion's hand energetically, he ran with him toward the floor of the narrow valley.

In the blink of an eye, the two men, passing through the bushes and thickets like cannonballs, reached the edge of the woods, but they came to a sudden halt, gripped by amazement and horror.

They had a frightful spectacle before their eyes. In the center of a vast clearing, on the banks of a stream hidden between two hedges of plants and bushes, forty hideous savages were surrounding a young woman of their own race, tightly bound to the trunk of a palm tree.

Standing in front of her, the man who seemed to be the chief of the tribe was armed with a large stone and some kind of tool, probably made of hard wood, reminiscent of an ice-pick. He applied the point of that instrument to the young woman's front teeth, and struck the other end with all his might. The victim uttered a terrible scream, like the ones the two friends had heard, and a stream of blood ran from her mouth over her breast, which was decorated with strange tattoos.

A roar of approval uttered by the audience demonstrated that the operation had succeeded, and the youngest of the savages plunged his fingers into the patient's mouth, to pull out three or four broken teeth.

At that sight, Marcel felt his hair standing on end, but Trinitus, recalling the customs of Oceanic peoples, reassured his friend.

"It's a marriage," he told him. "We're at a wedding! Let's get out of here!"

Suddenly, a shrill clamor, as piercing as the call of a bird of prey, resounded behind the clumps of laurels and canna in which the two friends were hidden.

Terrified by that unexpected attack they turned round, and saw a human form passing through the trees like lightning, which immediately disappeared.

"Run!" cried Trinitus. "We've been seen!"

Breathlessly, pray to the sharpest fear, Marcel emerged from hiding. The two companions, holding their guns at the ready, accelerating their progress and bending down to stay out of sight of the indigenes, beat a retreat toward the coast, trying to get back to their boat.

At the cry of alarm they had heard, however, the natives busy with the cruel ceremony that had excited Marcel's indignation were gripped by a kind of panic terror, and, untying the young woman in order to reunite her with her fiancé, they ran off, shouting, to fetch weapons from the huts they had constructed in the depths of the valley.

Some of the savages lived in caves hollowed out in the sides of the hill, others contented themselves with cabins constructed with banana leaves, but they all possessed formidable weapons. Axes of shaped flint, assegais, clubs, knives improvised from natural splinters of jasper and porphyry, arrows made from sharp stones fixed to hardwood stems: the entire arsenal dating in Europe from the Stone Age was in the savages' hands.

When they ran into the village, shouting and gesticulating madly in a hundred strange fashions, all their fellows, who had not quit their huts, armed themselves in haste and mingled with the newcomers. In the blink of an eye, the entire tribe was in motion, like an agitated ant-hive. The men picked up axes and assegais, the women and children armed themselves with pointed sticks and large stones. Two columns formed, each composed of more than sixty combatants, and while one went along the river-bank to cut off the enemy's retreat, the other raced into the woods in pursuit of the fugitives.

Soon, Trinitus and Marcel, having scarcely covered a quarter of the distance they needed to travel in order to get back to the *Éclair*, could hear a distant rumor behind them—but the sinister noise was becoming louder and more distinct with every passing second. It was like a storm wind blowing through the wood; at intervals, louder shouts rose above it, mingled with the crackle of broken branches.

"Run! Run!" cried Trinitus, out of breath—but a sudden murmur, as deep and muffled as the one he had just heard, struck his ear again.

Amazed, the two companions stopped and looked at one another, gripped by fear. The second murmur was coming from the direction of the sea.

"We're surrounded!" said Marcel, darting anxious glances around him. Pale and terrified, he was about to lean against a tree when an idea of genius traversed Trinitus' mind, and the latter grabbed his young companion's arm.

"Come on! Come on!" he cried to him, and, racing through the bushes and thickets, he dragged his companion to the edge of one of the deep ravines hollowed out in the side of the hill by the rain. The walls of the broad crevice, three or four meters high, were almost vertical.

Marcel, not knowing whether he was about to fall into a snake-pit, hesitated momentarily, but, shoved by Trinitus, he leapt into the abyss with him.

Fortunately, there was a thick layer of sand at the bottom of the ravine. The two fugitives got to their feet in haste, and Trinitus, observing on the opposite wall of the gulf a mass of rock laid bare by the waters, under which there was a profound fissure, resolved to make a fortress against their assailants. He climbed up to it precipitately with Marcel, shoved two boulders under the rock that had been detached from it, heaped a few other large stones on to that initial base, and rapidly constructed a wall pierced with loopholes, behind which he and Marcel took cover. From the foot of that rampart to the bottom of the ravine, the steeply-inclined bank formed a natural fortification, and that was the only direction from which an attack was possible.

Trinitus was no longer seeking to reassure Marcel

now. He did not hesitate to tell him that, of all the dangers they had run, this was the greatest. The indigenes armed against them appeared to belong to the family of Alfourous[10] or Melanesians, the most ferocious of all the tribes populating the Pacific islands. It would be a hundred times better to die fighting them than to fall into their hands alive.

At that supreme moment, the two friends thought about the two beloved women whom cruel destiny seemed to be removing increasingly further from their route, and, gathering all their courage to vanquish the emotion that gripped them, prepared themselves for the battle.

Meanwhile, a terrible clamor, accompanied by frightful laughter, cries of joy and sinister chants, told them that the savages were on their track. In fact, the two bands had just met up again, and, guided by the dire instinct that animated them, they were marching tumultuously toward the ravine where Trinitus and Marcel had taken refuge.

---

10. The term "Alfourou" was used by several nineteenth-century proto-anthropologists, including William Charles Martin and James Cowles Pritchard to refer to the indigenes of Australia, New Guinea and Polynesia, which were held by those writers to constitute the most primitive of the human racial types. Although obsolete, it still crops up occasionally in French popular fiction in the twentieth century, perhaps borrowed from Rengade.

# CHAPTER NINETEEN
## THE BATTLE

Having arrived in the presence of the rock under which the fugitives were sheltered, the horrible troop of Alfourous came to a sudden halt.

The ravine separated them from the retrenchment that protected the two companions, but the ferocious indigenes recognized very quickly that the two men they were looking for were hidden behind the blocks of stone. One of them even discovered the path they had carved out through the middle of the plants growing in the ravine, and, gazing intently, saw Trinitus' ardent eyes glittering through the interstices of the improvised rampart. In response to his call, all the heads leaned over to look and all the hands extended to point at the enemy and threaten them.

The entire troop, composed of a hundred and fifty-two individuals, came to form a group at the place from which they had the best view of the rock, and without any order, decision or command, the howling multitude prepared for battle.

The Alfourous, as several voyagers have observed, are highly skilled in making use of axes and clubs; they also know how to make artful use of the slingshot, and some of them shoot arrows and throw assegais with great dexterity.

The majority of those who had come to lay siege to Trinitus and Marcel were armed with clubs or axes, but among their number the scientist saw several who were carrying bows or javelins, and he pointed them out to his companion.

"Those are the most dangerous," he told him. "Their weapons are poisoned with curare.[11] We need to begin with them."

Suddenly, a hail of stones launched from the opposite edge of the ravine began to rain down on the rock, sending numerous splinters flying from the crest of the wall. A few projectiles even rebounded into the grotto through a large opening above the rampart, but they did not injure Trinitus or Marcel.

In order to conserve the element of surprise, the scientist did not want to respond to that initial attack, and, thinking that the stones would be followed by arrows, he warned Marcel in order that they could open fire at the same moment on the bowmen who presented themselves.

More cunning than Trinitus thought, however, the others understood that they were wasting their time and their weapons firing at the wall. They had seen that the only issue open to projectiles was the large space separating the rock from the upper part of the rampart, and that it was by way of that opening—a veritable chink

---

11. Curare is a South American poison; the various plants from which it can be extracted are not native to Vanuatu.

in the armor—that they resolved to launch their arrows and assegais. An enormous mangrove tree leaning over the ravine, whose colossal branches extended like a natural bridge all the way to the rock, seemed to have been planted at the edge of the profound ditch to favor that perfidious maneuver.

On seeing all the Alfourous armed with arrows gathering at the foot of that tree and disputing the glory of climbing up ahead of the others, Trinitus deduced their intentions and understood that by moving along the branches they would arrive directly over the rampart.

Fortunately, in spite of their agility, they could not all reach the crown of the tree and the same time, and Marcel did not despair of shooting them down as they arrived at the transversal branches.

Those natives who had nothing with which to attack or defend themselves but stone axes or clubs started uttering horrible cries, rolling in the sand, rubbing their bodies with ocher-tinted dirt and jumping pell-mell into the ravine in order to mount an assault on the grotto, while their companions, posted in the branches, peppered the besieged men with arrows.

At the sight of those horrible demons unleashed against them. Trinitus and Marcel shivered.

"You take those in the tree," the scientist said. "I'll take the others...."

And they both raised their guns.

There was a frightful moment of silence.

Roaring and screeching, the Alfourous had invaded the floor of the ravine, and were gazing with anxious ferocity, axes in hand, terrible and menacing, at those few piled-up stones that were almost within arm's reach, and behind which they could sense their palpitating prey.

Trinitus, violently excited, saw all those sparkling eyes, white teeth and tattooed faces turn toward him avidly, at a distance of a few feet beyond the sight of his gun; with a profound anxiety he studied the oily and shiny skulls, the bare panting torsos, advancing and rising up like a tide to reach the base of the rampart. The strong odor of all those hideously variegated bodies seized him by the throat; he could already smell the fetid breath of all those mouths, thirsty for human blood, and beneath his nervous finger, he pressed the trigger of his weapon, ready to fire.

Suddenly, a clamor even more frightful than the preceding ones resounded, and the head of the most courageous of the assailants appeared over the top of the rampart. Trinitus' rifle focused on him, and the shot was fired. The Alfourou, his skull shattered, collapsed without making a sound, and his frightened companions retreated abruptly, while Marcel, in his turn, shot a second enemy hiding in the branches of the tree.

Momentarily disconcerted by the death of their bravest warriors and by the detonation of the firearms, the Alfourous hesitated for a few seconds before mounting a new assault. Soon excited by the sight of the two corpses and the shouts of their chiefs, however, they rushed the rampart with a new impetuosity.

Fortunately for the besieged pair, the slope sustaining

the fortification was steep and rocky; it was difficult for more than two men to climb up at the same time, and Trinitus reloaded his weapon quickly enough to have two shots to fire at each climb. The assailants were killed every time; the bullets blew out their brains or passed through their torsos. They fell backwards like inert masses, crushing those who were assisting them and hastening after them.

The combatants armed with arrows were no more fortunate, and Marcel cut them down as soon as they ventured on to the branches of the tree.

The savages were no longer retreating, though. To every rifle-shot they replied with a roar of fury, and launched themselves forward, enraged, against the inaccessible wall. Their axes and pikes were impotent. Assegais and arrows also rained down on the rock, but the majority, hitting the stone, rebounded on to the heads of the attackers, only increasing their wrath and their disorder.

Suddenly, Marcel heard abrupt and precipitate sounds resounding at the base of the mangrove tree, and it was not difficult too deduce that the savages were striking it with their axes in order to send it tumbling into the ravine.

That was a clever maneuver on the part of the assailants, for the gigantic mangrove was leaning over directly above the rampart, and could not fail to bring it down as it fell. The height of the wall of ravine protected the Alfourous engaged in that work; it was impossible to hit them or disperse them with rifle-shots.

In response to a particular cry that they uttered, all those who were fighting in vain in the ravine suddenly moved off, passing from blind fury to the liveliest joy. Out of range of Trinitus' shots, they watched the enormous tree trembling above their heads, ready to fall upon the frail wall that all their efforts had not been able to breach.

It would be all over for Trintus and Marcel. Their forearms would become useless. In their despair, they resolved to allow themselves to be crushed by the branches of the tree rather than fall into the hands of the Alfourous alive.

Relentlessly attacked by twenty vigorous arms, the mangrove was oscillating with terrible creaks. Huddled close together, hand In hand, the besieged pair saw the formidable mass of verdure swaying over their heads, threatening to bury them. It was like an avalanche suspended overhead, and by a cruel irony, it was an avalanche of leaves and flowers.

The tree shuddered more and more. Frightful shocks shook its enormous branches and made a swarm of frightened butterflies take flight from the corollas. Insouciantly, intoxicated by perfumes, they fluttered away two by two, rising in spirals into the sky—and Marcel's glazed stare accompanied them until they disappeared into the shade of the wood. Trinitus, his head bowed and his eyes moist, held his young friend in his arms, awaiting the horrid fall that would crush them against the rock....

Finally, one last crack was heard, and, in the midst

of a deafening racket and tumult, the tree fell.

The Alfourous precipitated themselves into the ravine, which the mangrove filled with its vast branches, and stated singing a song of victory. The rampart had been demolished by the branches of the tree that had broken against the rock and scored it with profound grooves.

Although buried under the foliage, Trinitus and Marcel had not been crushed, and their injuries were limited to a few bruises. The Alfourous, hurrying to take their revenge, fell upon them, tore their garments into shreds, shared out their weapons, and, joyful on seeing that they were still breathing, bound them solidly with lianas and thongs.

Then a scene commenced which chilled the two prisoners with terror. A few Alfouours lit a big fire in the middle of the ravine, and Marcel was dragged by the ferocious cannibals to the edge of the blaze. Just as knives brought to red heat in the flames were approaching his tremulous limbs, however, twenty more savages ran up carrying a kind of stretcher made of tree branches, and shouting with all their might: "Koyauw! Koyauw!"

At that magic word, the most ferocious bowed down, touching their heads to sand, and, rising promptly to their feet again, helped to place the two half-dead captives on the stretcher. The Alfourous who had come to claim the victims loaded it on to their robust shoulders and, followed by all their companions, singing and dancing, headed toward the center of the island.

# CHAPTER TWENTY
## THE GOD

Lying side-by side on the narrow stretcher, tied up by solid thongs and bruised by the fall of the tree that the savages had brought down on top of them, Trinitus and Marcel were prey to the most frightful anguish.

They did not even have the strength to sustain one another reciprocally with a few words of hope and consolation; everything they could see and hear appeared to them to be a horrible nightmare. Frightful demons were carrying them off; ferocious clamors were resounding in their ears; a hundred hideous heads surrounded them, fixing oblique eyes upon them in which gleams of the most atrocious desire shone.

Where were they being taken? Why had they not been sacrificed right away? What refinement of cruelty was being prepared for their torture? Neither of them knew. They were prey and booty, and were under no illusion as to the fate that awaited them.

The Alfourous, alert and vigorous, were marching rapidly in spite of their burden. Some of the warriors following the stretcher helped the porters from time to time; others, uttering loud howls of joy, triumphantly ran ahead, clearing the way.

The country that the frightful caravan traversed was splendid. A thousand flowering shrubs embalmed the atmosphere with their sickly emanations; swarms of beetles were fluttering through the trees in all directions; magnolias with white flowers were filled with birds; the horizon, sometimes closed by a curtain of woodland, sometimes uncovered and drowned in the azure, presented the most picturesque appearances at every moment.

Trinitus regretted not having died in the ice of Victoria Land; he envied the fate of the unfortunate castaways of the *Jenny*, and the magnificence of the landscape that was offered to his gaze awoke in his soul an ardent desire to die. So, in order not to increase the anguish that was tormenting him with futile wishes, he closed his eyes to the ravishing spectacle that unfurled ironically around him.

It was not until after an hour's march that the Alfourous emerged from the woods into a valley traversed by a broad stream, and suddenly, on turning around a large clump of trees and gigantic grasses, a village appeared the base of a high hill, composed of some two or three hundred cabins.

As soon as the troop had been spotted the inhabitants of the village, a multitude of other indigenes, ran to see the prisoners and congratulate the combatants. The tumult and the shouting redoubled, and it was not without difficulty that the stretcher-bearers arrived at the entrance to the village, into a kind of small square shaded by palm trees. Beneath these trees was laid a large block of stone covered in a black crust exhaling a noxious odor, and over which a swarm of hungry flies were fluttering. It was a sacrificial altar, soiled with clotted blood. Some distance away from the horrible slab, on the black, charred soil, stood three or four other large stones, burned by fire and laden with a mass of wood and dried plants.

It was at the foot of that pyre that Trinitus and Marcel were deposited, but the scientist was the first to be carried to the slab, and before he was able to say a final adieu to his companion, he felt himself laid on the funereal altar. At the same time, an Alfourou set fire to a fragment of bark by rubbing it rapidly against a kind of wooden disk designed for that purpose, and carried it to the pyre.

A column of blue-tinted smoke rose into the air, and the ferocious clamors of all the indigenes arranged in a circle around the square announced to the victims that their torture was about to commence.

During that interval two sacrificers armed with stone knives and lancets carved in human bone had approached Trinitus. They had placed a cup beneath his head made from half of a coconut shell, but they seemed to be waiting with a keen anxiety for the arrival of the chief or God of the tribe before killing the prisoner.

The crowd was already getting impatient when and infernal music and cries, repeated a hundred times over, of "Koyauw! Koyauw!" finally announced the approach of the god. The circle of Alfourous opened on one side; all the savages prostrated themselves, lying face down, and on a kind of palanquin carried by eight indigenes, the Koyauw appeared. His body, daubed with red and blue, was clad in a long veil of yellow thread, and on his head a hat made of reeds and foliage formed a crude representation of the image of the sun.

The priests carrying the palanquin set it down gently in the middle of the square, and the god stood up. Suddenly, a cry of amazement and joy escaped his throat.

"Trinitus! Marcel!" he cried, half-mad with joy. And, seizing the sacrificer's knife, he cut the bonds securing the two captives.

The two men, awakened as if from a dream, got to their feet mechanically, and stared, utterly bewildered, at their liberator, who was prevented from speaking by great emotion. Then, suddenly recognizing him under his frightful disguise, they both pronounced the same name simultaneously.

"Nicaise!"

And, with their eyes bathed in tears, they threw themselves into the arms of their old companion.

Before going any further, it is perhaps indispensable to tell the reader how Nicaise had acquired the rank of supreme god among the savages.

You will doubtless remember the formidable battle engaged in the Coral Sea between a narwhal and a whale. Only heeding his courage, Nicaise had descended on to the swing placed beneath the boat, and after having launched his electric harpoon he had disappeared, doubtless carried off by the two enormous combatants.

This is what had happened: the narwhal, hit by the harpoon, had abruptly turned around, and it tusk had gone clean through Nicaise's impermeable garment. Transpierced in that fashion, but without being wounded, the latter had been snatched from his seat and carried for a great distance under the sea by the mortally-wounded unicorn. The small quantity of air contained in the diving-suit in which Nicaise was clad had sufficed to preserve him from asphyxia, but he had fallen unconscious and dragged by the narwhal, without having any suspicion of it, all the way to the Alfourous' island, where he had run aground with it on the coast.

As chance would have it, at that very moment, the indigenes were celebrating the great festival of the sun on the sea shore. At the sight of the unicorn, which had brought a human body from the bottom of the sea in a sort of canvas bag suspended from its tusk, the Alfourous had no doubt that the package was addressed to them. They believed that it was a gift from the star they were worshipping, and when they had stripped Nicaise of his living apparatus, they took him home with them, with a common accord, and, entirely naturally, rendered him all divine honors.

Poor Nicaise, waking up in the midst of those horrible savages, who were crowding around him, was somewhat surprised at first, but because he soon understood, on perceiving the cadaver of the narwhal, the strange voyage that he had just made, he rapidly deduced that he was being taken, if not for a god, at least for a superb object of curiosity.

Furthermore, he was overwhelmed by excellent care and attention; his slightest gesture inspired terror, and when, after one or two anthrophagic dinners in which he was obliged to take part, he had realized what kind of people he was dealing with, he told himself philosophically that it was better to be their idol than to serve as their beefsteak.

Let us now return to our story.

The Alfourous, momentarily surprised by the strange attitude of their god in the presence of the two prisoners, did not take kindly to that scene of tenderness, and demanded the sacrifice of the victims with angry roars. In spite of the power that he had over the tribe, Nicaise trembled for his friends and wondered with the greatest anxiety how he was going to save them from the fury of the cannibals.

Suddenly, however, he had an inspiration of genius. Perceiving that the sun, already in decline, was about to disappear behind thick clouds that were rising at the horizon, he harangued the hideous populace that surrounded him, making them understand that it was necessary not to sacrifice the victims at the moment when the sun was setting. The presence of the sun was indispensable to the ceremony, and it was the following day, at dawn, that it was necessary to present it with the magnificent offering.

Confronted by these important reasons, the Alfourous gave in—which they probably would not have done had they been civilized. Superstition triumphed over gluttony, and the sacrificers, dropping their knives, approached Trinitus and Marcel.

"Let them do as they wish," said Nicaise to his friends. "It would be dangerous for me to appear to protect you any further. They're going to tie you to the trunk of a palm tree, but that won't do you any harm.

The sacrificers approached and tied up the prisoners, who were only partly reassured, in spite of Nicaise's inexplicable authority.

"Ten armed men will stay with you," the god continued. "In a few hours, after nightfall, they'll be brought a whitish beverage in clay cups, which might be offered to you. Be certain not to touch it—it will be poison. Shortly thereafter, I'll come to cut your bonds, and we'll leave without being seen...."

"The *Éclair*'s waiting for us on the coast," Trinitus replied.

A gleam of joy illuminated Nicaise's eyes, but the old mariner, striving to contain the emotion that was choking him, climbed back on to his palanquin with a theatrical gravity that would have made Trinitus and Marcel burst out laughing in any other circumstances.

The high priests loaded their divinity religiously on to their shoulders and the square slowly emptied, while the two prisoners, bound close together, exchanged a few words in low voices and felt hope reborn in their souls, so cruelly tortured for so long.

Meanwhile, the clouds rose into the sky and darkness fell rapidly. The atmosphere was heavy, the heat overwhelming, gusts of wind made the leaves quiver, and dull rumbles of thunder resounded in the atmosphere.

The Alfourous responsible for standing guard over the two captives were sitting around the pyre, which ended up dying down, and, while waiting until they could roast Trinitus and Marcel, they regaled themselves with little freshwater turtles, which they ate almost raw.

# CHAPTER TWENTY-ONE
## THE FLIGHT

The god Nicaise, very happy, as can be imagined, to have found hid friends again, was not thinking about anything but their liberation and taking flight with them. His "temple," a heavy and massive hut made of reed palisades and clods of turf, was not very comfortable, and he preferred the hat daubed with the aureole of the anthropophagic Jupiter.

At any rate, it was very easy to put into execution the formidable project that he had conceived. He alone was to prepare the beverage for the victims and the guards, and he had at his disposal in the temple the juices and venous extracts of which the savages made use to poison their weapons. So, as soon as he judged the moment favorable, he extracted a clear pink liquid from a vast earthenware vat and poured it into two large pitchers. As he had no fear that the Alfouorous could read French, he wrote the word *Poison* on the sides of the pitchers.

Then, taking a little packet the size of his fist from a crack in the wall, he unrolled the long dry leaf in which it was wrapped, broke the reddish substance it contained into fragments, and threw all the fragments into the two pitchers. At that moment, however, his hand trembled and his legs felt weak. The beverage was going to kill ten men, and Nicaise felt anxious that he was about to commit a great crime. The storm that was rumbling outside completed the augmentation of his fear, and the poor god wondered, as he looked in horror at the two full vessels, whether he sought find another means of salvation.

Suddenly, having not found any, he seized the two pitchers and handed them to an Alfourou who was on watch in a kind of vestibule adjacent to the hut. The latter prostrated himself and, laden with the sacred beverage, headed for the palm trees in the midst of which Trinitus and Marcel were tied up.

The wind had risen considerably; for several hours it had been heard rumbling in the nearby forests, and the clouds were increasingly heaping up over the Alfourou tribe. It was not raining yet, but, judging by the intensity of the lightning-flashes, which were succeeding one another with frightening rapidity, the two captives were expecting a terrible tempest. They were glad about that, moreover, being convinced that the storm would protect their flight and hide the traces of their footprints from their enemies.

Suddenly, a flash of lightning dissipating the nocturnal obscurity showed the Alfourous guarding the victims that their god had not forgotten them. The man to whom Nicaise had confided the two pitchers had just arrived in the sacrificial square, and two seconds later, his companions were greeting him with cries of joy. At the sight of the sinister messenger, Trinitus and Marcel felt their courage weakening, but on reading the word *poison* written on the cups by the light of the fire they thought gladly that the moment of their deliverance was drawing near.

The Alfourou offered them the pitcher ceremoniously, and, untroubled by their refusal, he handed both pitchers to the guards with a smile. The latter sat down around the fire and, one after another, they drank delightedly, until the liquid was gone.

The indigene sent by Nicaise took the empty pitchers and disappeared.

Then the two captives witnessed a frightful spectacle. After a few minutes, five or six Alfourous stood up simultaneously, like specters, and, mouths agape, their eyes immobilized in their orbits, their necks stiff, their arms violently throw backwards, their legs tortured by frightful cramps, fell backwards as if struck dead. The others hardly had time to utter a hoarse exclamation; seized by the same symptoms, creased and contracted by the same convulsions, they writhed on the ground in frightful anguish. Some, killed at a stroke by that horrible tetanus, lay there supported only by their head and heels, their twisted bodies forming a semicircular arch. The fire, incessantly revived by the wind, and the numerous flashes of lightning that rent the sky, illuminated the frightful scene.

Marcel closed his eyes in fright. Trinitus, amazed, forgot that he was bound and recognized with horror, by the hideous contractions of the bodies deformed by the poison, the terrible effects of strychnine.

Suddenly, a friendly voice was heard a few paces away in the darkness.

"Trinitus! Marcel"

"Nicaise!" replied the prisoners, overwhelmed by joy.

Almost immediately, their bonds were broken and they found themselves in their old companion's arms.

"Lets go, quickly!" said the latter. "The moment is very favorable, but we have many hours of walking ahead of us to get to the sea."

"We'll arrive before daybreak," said Marcel.

"I can guide you reliably to the ravine where you were take prisoner, and I hope that you'll be able to find your way from there."

"I'll answer for that, my dear Nicaise," Trinitus replied.

And the three companions, delighted to have found one another again so miraculously, promptly traversed the valley by the light of lightning flashes, to disappear into the profound darkness that bathed the high forest trees.

Almost at the same instant, the storm burst over the Alfourou tribe and the rain began to fall in torrents. The savages, huddled in their huts and terrified by the thunderbolts, invoked the protection of their Koyauw, little suspecting that he was traveling across country in such weather. The cadavers of the guards lying in the square of sacrifices were soon covered by a shroud of sand and mud.

The three fugitives had scarcely got into the woods when the tempest was unleashed in all its violence. In an instant, in spite of the protective vault of trees, the shreds of the garments that remained to them were inundated by the rain and their limbs were streaming. The joy they experienced in being free gave them strength, however, and all three of them, brisk and cheerful, ran like hares through the woodland. Soon, Nicaise—who found time to tell his story while fleeing —was even being assailed by gibes and jokes.

It is true that the old mariner, still coiffed on his emblematic sun, the splayed rays of which sheltered him like an umbrella, had the pitiful appearance of a king of fairyland harassed by some malevolent genie.

Trinitus, who was no longer calling him anything but Nicaise-Apollo, made the remark to him that his sun was dissolving and was scratching its rays on the branches of all the trees. Marcel implored him to make the tempest cease, and, when his prayers were unanswered, sent him to bed…in the bosom of Thetis.

The god contented himself with relying with bursts of laughter, and hastened to stride over the brushwood, saying that there was no time more propitious to desert his temple than one when the star that he represented could not see him.

The storm redoubled in intensity, however, and lightning strikes were falling continually upon the culminating points of the island. Two or three fires lit in the woods made red patches against the black sky of the horizon, and the atmosphere was so charged with electricity that luminous feathers were springing from the treetops and rocky spurs. The fugitives could see their route perfectly solely by the glare of the lightning; their ears were deafened by the resounding rumbling of the thunder and the din of the storm-wind in the forest.

It was thus that they reached the ravine in which Trinitus and Marcel had fought the Alfourous, but in that place a new sound mingled with the roar of the storm. It was a grave and sonorous voice, a profound and muted murmur, something as frightening and terrible as the furious breath of a new element that was coming to take part in the battle of the atmosphere and the fire.

The three men stopped at the same time, alarmed by the same thought.

That formidable noise was the sound of the sea rising. What would become of the boat that Trinitus had left moored on the coast?

Gripped by a sudden terror at that frightful idea, the fugitives raced in the direction of the sea. This time, the breathless Trinitus guided his two companions, and they, so insouciant and courageous a little while before felt the rain chilling their limbs.

They went rapidly down the slope of the hill that inclined toward the Ocean, and arrived on the shore almost at the same time. The furious waves were unfurling with unusual violence and breaking on the shore. In some places, the cliff, undermined by the waves, had crumbled into the sea, and the trees beneath which Trinitus had moored the *Éclair* no longer existed.

Not seeing any trace of his boat, the scientist uttered a cry of despair and rage, and Marcel fell to his knees on the sand, exhausted. As for Nicaise, he clenched his fists and ground his teeth in fury, muttering the sinister words: "We're doomed!"

It was necessary to make a rapid decision, however; at every moment the impetuous waves were sweeping over the beach and the three men were in great danger.

There was a kind of cruel and grim satisfaction in the anger of the waves. The Ocean, which had tried twenty times over, but always in vain, to break or submerge the *Éclair*, seemed proud to have done it in the end. Unable to swallow her in kelp, imprison her in its abysses, drown her in its whirlpools, strangle her with its ice or have her crushed by its monsters, it had stolen her treacherously by night, snatching her away from the coast, doubtless in order to smash her against some unknown shore.

Dazed, shivering and weeping with anger, Trinitus searched for his boat in vain. All around him there was darkness and desolation, and the luminous streaks of the lightning only served to show him the frightful power of the Ocean. The abyss had its prey, and was challenging Trinitus to come and retrieve it. The scientist could wring his hands and gaze imploringly as much as he wanted, but as soon as he moved nearer, the insulting waves spat foam at him, while the wind, impregnated with salt water, blew in his face, and the brutal water struck him in the chest and knocked him over.

Finally, after several hours of futile research, the fugitives, harassed by fatigue, were obliged to seek shelter. They went into a narrow valley buried under trees, and were fortunate enough to discover a rock carpeted with moss and ferns, under which they rested while waiting for daylight.

Meanwhile, the storm gradually eased and the sea slowly became calm again. When the sun appeared on the horizon, however, Nicaise thought that it was his duty not to conceal from his friends the numerous dangers threatening them.

The island was extremely populous, and the Alfourous would not stop searching it until they had recovered their victims. As for his divine power, Nicaise assumed that it was lost, and that his worshipers would only take it into account by roasting him first.

# CHAPTER TWENTY-TWO
## IN THE NICK OF TIME

Nicaise was not mistaken in his funereal apprehensions. The retreat in which his friends thought themselves secure from the Alfourous would not remain unknown for long to the ferocious cannibals, stimulated by the desertion of their god, the flight of their captives and the murder of their bravest warriors.

Two days after the escape, a group of indigenes recognized footprints in the sand on the sea-shore, and as Trinitus and his companions had been obliged to emerge from their hiding place to gather fruits and fresh water, it was not difficult to find traces of them in the valley where they were living.

So, on the morning of the third day, they were attacked by a hundred savages, who rushed at them with incredible fury.

All defense was futile. The three besieged men only had wooden sticks for weapons, and, during the first hail of stones launched by the Alfourous, Trinitus was hit in the head and fell to the ground face down, uttering a cry of pain.

Marcel tried to lift him up again, but the Alfourous

did not give him time. They charged, howling with rage at their vanquished enemies, and tied them up tightly.

Nicaise tried in vain to intimidate the crowd with his sacramental words. He only excited the sinister laughter of those who had previously trembled at his voice. Seized by the feet, he was dragged with his friends to the edge of the stream that was running through the valley.

The horrible shocks and jolts experienced by Trinitus brought him back to consciousness, but the unfortunate man only opened his eyes to witness the preparations for his long agony.

Rapidly, the Alfouous lit an enormous fire. They set about heating their large knives in the blaze, and, tying Nicaise to a tree-trunk first, started dancing a frenzied saraband around him. The poor god only had time to shake his friends' hands briefly and stammer a few words that his emotion rendered unintelligible.

Trinitus' and Marcel's eyes filled with tears; they looked at the sky in order not to see their friend's torture.

Suddenly, a cry of desolation and pain chilled them with fear and suspended the breath in their oppressed chests.

One of the red-hot stone knives had made a profound incision in Nicaise's arm.

The joyful clamors of the Alfourous succeeded their victim's plaint, and other knives taken from the fire were approaching the victim's face.

Suddenly, however, two abrupt detonations rang out

from the depths of the woods, and the man torturing Nicaise fell down, dead.

At the same time, a furious barking resounded in the trees and cries of "Go! Go! Attack!" reached the ears of the captives.

"Is it a dream?" exclaimed Trinitus. In the transport of his joy, he broke the bonds that were swathing him.

Five or six further detonations demonstrated that he was not mistaken.

"Friends! Friends!" shouted Nicaise, in his turn, forgetting his wound and his pain.

When four more Alfouous had bitten the dust, three enormous dogs bounded into the middle of the amazed and fearful troop, like pouncing tigers. The natives were instantly overtaken by panic terror. Abandoning their captives and their weapons, they fled in all directions.

Meanwhile, Trinitus had freed his friends from their bonds, and all three, drunk with joy and gratitude, ran toward their liberators.

The latter, who were ten in number, advanced in a compact troop from the bushes where they had mounted the ambush—but two of them, who were evidently women, in spite of their bizarre accoutrements, broke abruptly into a run and threw their arms around Trinitus' neck, weeping with joy.

That was too much emotion for the poor scientist. Tears of affection sprang from his eyes, and his lips were unable to pronounce the two cherished words that his heart was repeating incessantly: Alice! Thérèse!

Hugging his daughter and his wife, he covered their foreheads with tears and kisses.

In the meantime, Marcel and Nicaise threw themselves into the arms of those who had just snatched them from the jaws of death. They were none other than the passengers of the *Richmond* who had escaped the shipwreck with Trinitus' wife and daughter.

Among them was the surgeon Sir William Hervey, Thérèse's cousin, whose joy was inexpressible, and whom the scientist embraced effusively, like a beloved brother.

The happiest of all, however, was Marcel, when he received Alice's thanks. How quickly he forgot, in her presence, the horrible danger he had been in!

His delight complete, Trinitus thought at times that he was dreaming. He could not account for the unexpected arrival of his liberators, and, trembling at the thought that the beautiful illusion might vanish, he dared not ask any question on that subject.

Sir William's voice extracted him from his ecstasy. "Our boats are waiting on the coast," the surgeon said. "Let's hurry to get back to home. The Alfourous have only to rise up *en masse* to crush us."

"You have a home?" asked Trinitus, astonished.

"Yes indeed! A few miles over the sea—an entire island, which we have conquered at swordspoint.

Nicaise and Marcel were no less agreeably surprised than Trinitus when they learned this good news.

"And how did you learn that we were in the midst of these cannibals?" asked the scientist.

"Haven't you guessed?" said Alice, smiling. "Your bizarre boat was washed up on the coast of our island by the tempest, and it ran aground almost at my feet. I was with Maman and Sir William. We were quite astonished at first, on seeing that enormous machine, but when it collided with the rocks it had split, and a host of objects had spilled out on to the sand. I saw a few papers, ran to pick them up, and read: *the Éclair, Captain Trinitus...*. The last line of the manuscript read: "*We are disembarking east of New Caledonia on an island that might be Anatom in the New Hebrides. O joy! You were nearby! And...*""

Emotion prevented the young woman from finishing her sentence. Trinitus, overcome once again by tenderness, hugged his dear child in his arms.

"And you came to snatch us from the most horrible death!" he continued. "To die without seeing you again...my Thérèse, my Alice! That was my only fear, the unique preoccupation torturing my mind!"

"We searched the island for two days without being able to find you," Sir William went on. "The Alfourous have been cleverer than we were."

"It was the smoke of the fire that put us on their track," added one of the Richmond's passengers.

"And the noses of our dogs," another put in.

"Plock did well," interjected a third. "He hunts Alfourous like hares."

"It required prodigies to help us rid our island of natives," said the oldest of the company in his turn, "and God knows how much trouble we had putting an end to them."

"I can easily believe it," observed Marcel, two whom Alice's beautiful eyes were giving heart. "Hunt the native and he comes back at the gallop!"

"Bravo!" replied Sir William. "But let's get back aboard in a hurry, in case the natives offer further evidence for the proverb. It's necessary not to play games with people who understand diplomatic language so well."

"You're telling me!" said Nicaise. "I've been their good god for a week, and this morning, paying no heed to my head-dress, representative of the sun that they worship, they were about to cut me into slices."

"You've been a god?" queried Sir William and his companions.

"As you see me now," said Nicaise, "three days ago I was painted like an *image d'Épinal*…red, green and blue feathers. I looked like a parrot. But the rain the other night washed my colors away. I was a false god! What can you expect?"

Chatting in that manner, they reached the shore where the boats had been moored. They were three long canoes imitative of the savages' pirogues, but much better constructed; the handiwork of intelligent and civilized workers was recognizable therein.

The three dogs that had returned from hunting Alfourous a few moments before, their mouths bloody, were the first to leap into the boats, and a few minutes later, the *Richmond*'s passengers took their new friends to the island that they had conquered.

They disembarked in a shady inlet in the depths of a delightful bay formed by the mouth of a wide stream. Trinitus perceived an enormous metallic sphere under a clump of mimosas, broken and battered but recognizable without difficulty. It was the debris of the *Éclair*.

In a vast meadow there were several goats, which Sir William and the other castaways had captured in the mountains while very young and had succeeded in domesticating.

At the end of the vast green expanse, where the island's flora was displayed in al its magnificence, drowned in the banana-trees and laurier-roses, was the villa constructed by the new inhabitants. They had named it Valfleury.

Alice and Thérèse explained to Trinitus and his companions how they were cultivating and making use of that vast domain. The island was exceedingly fertile, and rich harvests could be obtained without a great deal of difficulty.

The woods that covered the side of the mountain beyond Valfeury furnished fruits and game in abundance, and miraculous catches could be obtained by fishing in the mouth of the river. A few rocks on the coast were laden with oysters, for the benefit of gourmets.

Sir William's botanical knowledge had been very useful, and, thanks to him, the villa possessed a splendid garden.

Finally, after walking for half an hour, the caravan reached Valfleury. The most elegant of the three cabins making up the hamlet was reserved for Thérèse and Alice. It was a nest buried under climbing plants and covered by the protective shade of gigantic palm trees. A multitude of birds with fiery plumage were playing in the sunlight; in the courtyard, and heaped up in a hangar was equipment for cultivation, hunting and fishing.

Trinitus, Nicaise, and Marcel thought that they were in the Earthly Paradise. Marcel, most of all, was beginning to have charming dreams.

A week ago, moreover, the island had ceased to be a prison. A steamer bound for the Marquesas Islands would take the castaways of the *Richmond* aboard on its imminent return journey to France.

In the intoxication of his happiness, Trinitus did not forget to complete Marcel's. He divined very rapidly that his young friend had touched Alice's heart, and when he obtained that confession from the dear child, he immediately ran to find the man who had so courageously shared his tribulations and misfortunes.

That day, Marcel was working in the garden. Smiling, Trinitas took him to his daughter, and a few moments later, the delighted young man was holding Alice's hand tenderly.

# ABOUT THE TRANSLATOR

**BRIAN STABLEFORD** has translated more than a hundred volumes of French prose into English. His principal interests are the French Romantic Movement and its Decadent/Symbolist aftermath, with particular reference to the evolution of the *conte cruel*, and the evolution of the *roman scientifique* from its origins in the eighteen-century *conte philosophique* to the aftermath of the Great War of 1914-18.